I0712554

WRITE THAT DOWN

JAMI ROGERS

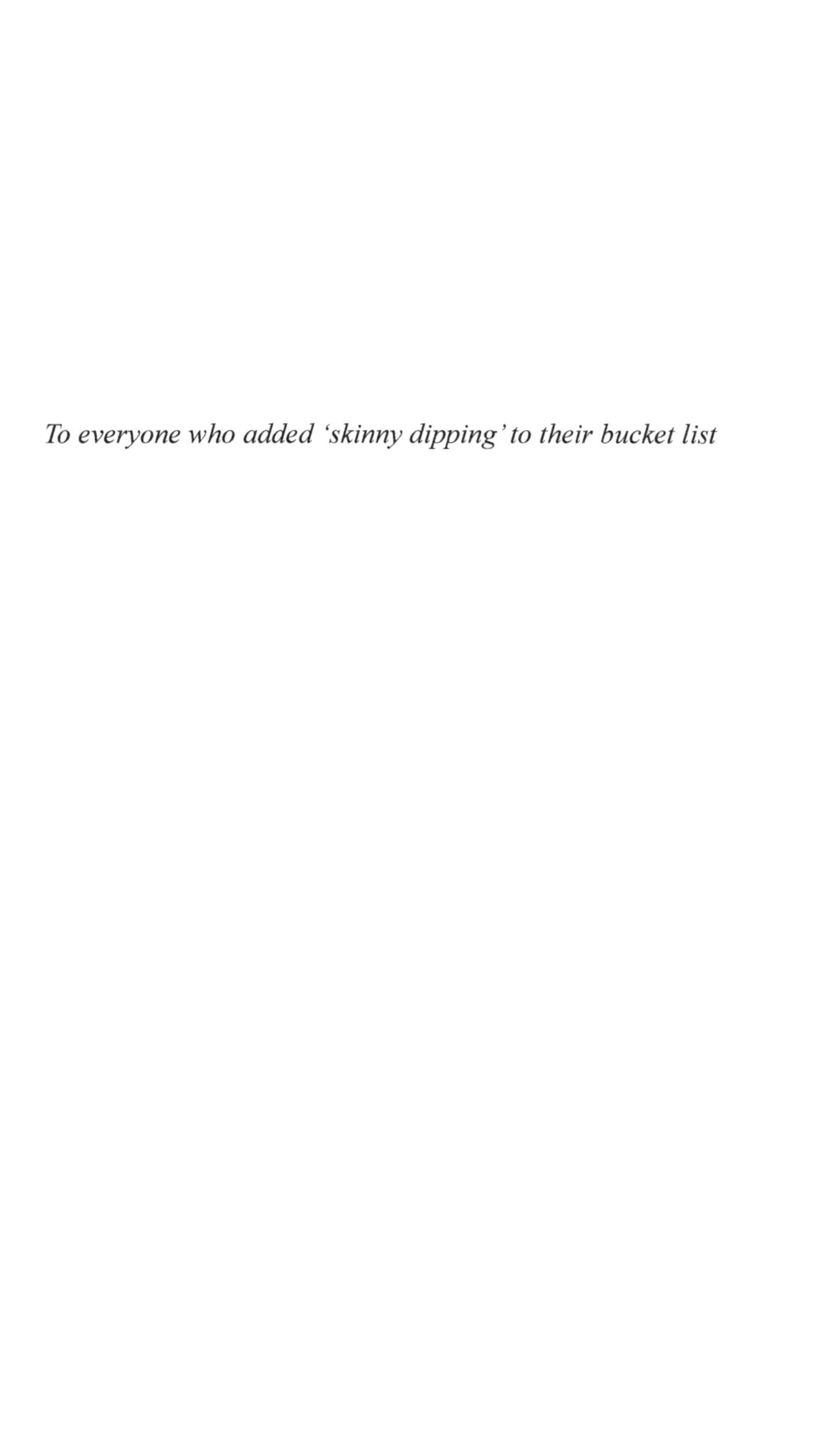

To everyone who added 'skinny dipping' to their bucket list

Copyright © 2023 by Jami Rogers
All rights reserved.

No part of this book may be used for AI learning or generation, reproduced or transmitted in any form or by any means, electronic or mechanical, including photocopying, recording, or by any information storage and retrieval system without the author's written permission, except for the use of brief quotations in a review.

This is a work of fiction. Names, characters, businesses, places, events and incidents are either the products of the author's imagination or used in a fictitious manner. Any resemblance to actual persons, living or dead, or actual events is purely coincidental.

Cover design © Hang Le byhangle.com

Elements Cover Design by Erika Plum Designs

Editor: Julie Sturgeon, CEO Editor, ceoeditor.com

Proofreading: Owl Eyes Proof and Edits, www.owleyesproofsedits.com

Visit my website: www.authorjamirogers.com

Formatted with Vellum

WRITE THAT DOWN

JAMI ROGERS

CHAPTER ONE
GRAHAM

Holy shit, I'm doing it.

I rise from the desk in my room at Lovers Lodge Resort and close my laptop.

Sitting here by myself on a perfectly good Friday night is what I always do. My life is like the back of a shampoo bottle. Rinse and repeat. My days are filled with waking up at 5:00 a.m. on the dot, working out for an hour, eating a clean breakfast, and then I write. I write a few thousand words, do some admin writer's work, and then I take care of daily human tasks such as cleaning, cooking, grocery shopping, hanging out with friends and so on throughout the days, followed by another two thousand words in the evening before I go to bed. Every. Single. Day. The only thing that changes each day is what I do in my afternoons.

Shit, I even kept my schedule during my last vacation in Nashville. While the guys were ordering shots and singing loudly along with the live band, I was standing in the corner of Tootsies rooftop bar, typing scenes out in a Google doc on my phone. It didn't matter that Broadway was alive just a few floors down or that every bar on the block had different music playing that blurred together; I had words to write, and nothing was going to stop me.

Which brings me back to this moment right here. One of my best friends, Zane, just got engaged to his girlfriend, Willa, mere hours ago, and while our group of friends went to the resort's lounge to celebrate, I headed back to my room to get my nightly words in.

What is wrong with me?

Don't get me wrong—I love routine. I thrive off it. I can depend on it. It keeps the stress away.

But today, watching my friend propose a lifetime commitment, set my mind racing.

Will I meet someone?

Will I have a moment like that?

As a romance writer, of course, I hope I get my happily ever after. I do.

Obviously, my so-called perfect routine doesn't have a spot for me to meet someone. Single women aren't lining up at the self-checkout waiting for Mr. Right to walk in, I can assure you that.

No, it's not going to happen unless I get outside of my box.

I run a comb through my hair and add a little mousse to freshen up, and then I tuck my dress shirt back into my jeans, slipping my dockers on at the same time.

One would think that I'm going to find my friends. Grab a drink and toast to the new happy couple to be.

One would be wrong.

I'm stepping outside of my box.

Tonight, this choice doesn't include my friends.

The elevator dings at the main floor, and I slowly move in the direction of the largest ballroom. The resort has three.

I pause outside the door; the music playing hints that my chances of being just another guest walking in that no one pays attention to while everyone else is mingling about or dancing are high.

About an hour ago, I said I was doing this and chickened out. I went back to my room, but here I am. Back. Ready to … I have no clue.

Just go in, find a corner, and blend in.

I step inside before I can stop myself.

I tug at the collar of my crisp white button-down shirt and let out a breath as heat creeps into my neck.

I'm tucked away in a corner of the room where I'm pretty darn positive no one will notice me. Then again, I'm not the only one in the corner, so I'm sure someone has spotted me at this point.

My gaze sweeps the room, falling on giant centerpieces of white flowers and gold candles that will probably never be lit. Judging by the fact that every table has a candle with a different size and shape, it's a safe assumption. I bet they plan to resell them once the big night is over.

I let out of breath, studying the ball of white and black on the dance floor. Two people I've never met. In fact, I don't think I've actually seen their faces yet either.

I'm crashing a wedding.

Me. Graham Wright. Crashing a freaking wedding.

Oh. God.

I didn't just step out of my box. I blew the top off.

Breathe.

Someone is going to see me and notice that I snuck into this room. One look at me and they will see I do not belong here.

Maybe I should eat some cake? Or do something, anything other than just stand here.

It's really freaking hot in this banquet room.

Instead of just tugging at the collar of my shirt, I unbutton the top two buttons.

I'd take my jacket off, but where would I put it? What if I need to make a getaway and I forget my jacket, and someone traces it back to me?

I take one more breath.

What even is the point of crashing a wedding to just stand here and watch? If I'm not going to do anything other than silently have a panic attack in the corner, I may as well leave.

I take one step and stop.

If I leave, what was the whole purpose of doing this?

The purpose is, I'm in a rut. I'm a single guy, and I have a great career, and yet, both are missing something. They are missing the next step.

I do the same thing day in and day out. I drink the same green tea every morning. I order the same black coffee with two Splendas at my hometown coffee shop, and I always, *always* get a slice of lemon bread.

I like consistency. I like discipline.

Beck, a good friend and writing critique partner, once told me that if I want something different, I need to do something different. Hence, crashing a wedding.

Did I skip a few options? Sure. There are plenty of other things I could have chosen to start with. I could have talked to the cute redhead at the gym who can squat more than me. I could have signed up for a dating app. I could actually make eye contact with someone at the coffee shop and start a conversion. Nope. I decided to go all-out. I made a choice, and instead of dwelling on the worst possible outcome, I just went through with it.

Maybe I'll start tomorrow.

No, no. The old me would have bailed, so yeah, I'm staying put. Besides, no one here knows who I am. I won't see anyone in this room ever again, and I'm—

"Are you doing all right? Do you need to sit down?"

I clear my throat, and my neck pops when I turn to the soft voice.

"Shit," I say and cup the right side of my neck. My eyes pinch together as if that's going to make the pain vanish quicker.

"Oh, yikes, sorry. I didn't mean to startle you."

I rub my neck and let out a breath.

"It's not your fault I'm on edge."

"Oh," her voice raises an octave. "Please, do tell me why you're on edge at this lovely, lovely wedding."

The second *lovely* is filled with sarcasm, and it makes me smile. If anyone were to call me out, I'd want it to be someone who clearly isn't that impressed to be here.

Then again, she doesn't need the whole story, and the explanation for why I'm crashing a wedding is too much back-story on my life. After this night, I'll never see her again. No sense in getting too deep.

"It's a long story," I say and finally open my eyes to view the dance floor instead of looking at the woman next to me, who clearly wants to have a conversation. From the corner of my eye, I see her lean toward me.

"Are you secretly in love with the bride?"

I shake my head. "No."

"The groom?"

I chuckle. "Nah, his hair is too long for me."

I finally turn to face my newfound friend, and my next breath nearly chokes me.

Her silky chocolate-brown hair shines under the ballroom light, even under the pins that hold it back, and her skin is perfectly tanned. I'm a tall guy at six feet, but there is no doubt she reaches five ten, maybe five eleven. I glance at her feet and spot her heels. Okay, maybe five nine. She's fit. Her lips are a deep red. The color pairs perfectly with her black one-shoulder skintight top and light pink pleated maxi skirt.

Wow. Talk about observant. I've never studied a woman this much upon meeting her. Ever. And don't get me started on the pleated maxi skirt. I have three sisters. It's impossible to grow up in a house with three girls and not know these things. Especially as the youngest of the bunch.

Her head tilts back in an elegant way as she laughs, the sound soft and sweet. Almost as if she's had years of practice containing it.

"Are you here on the bride's side or the groom's side?" she asks, her gaze finding mine, and again, I'm taken aback. Her bright green eyes swallow me up and captivate every brain cell I own.

She smiles slowly, and I shake my head.

"Considering I've never met you, I'm sure it's the opposite of why you're here."

I have no idea where that came from, but it sounded great. It was quick and clever. I can thank a decade of writing romantic comedies for that one.

"Oh, I don't know either of them," she smiles at me and winks.

That was smooth.

I'm not sure if she's joking or not.

So I wink back. "Me either."

Another smile touches her lips, this one a little bigger than the one before it, but she quickly clears her throat and nods toward the man and woman of the hour.

"High school sweethearts or second chance love?"

"What?" The word comes out in almost a whisper. Does she know who I am? You don't just ask a random man about romance tropes unless you think he knows them. Most men don't.

"Umm," I stutter.

"Relax, it was a joke. I didn't expect you to answer."

"Second chance," I say quickly, as if I need to prove her wrong. "Longtime childhood friends who rekindled their love when they bumped into each other in college at his frat party. He was a known player, and she was quiet. Not exactly a book kind of girl, but she's always known her worth."

The woman next to me presses her lips together and nods before she smiles. "I like that. He fell first, of course," she adds.

"Naturally."

"His friends all loved her the first moment she put him in his place."

I nod. "And her friends warned her away from him till they saw how happy he made her."

The perfect laugh surrounds me once again.

"I'm Alice."

She offers her hand.

"Graham."

"Graham," she repeats slowly. The way it rolls off her tongue gives me chills.

Good chills, to be more specific. Like the kind of chills you get right before you do something crazy.

I watch her for a moment. In the mere five minutes I've spent with her, I already know I want to spend more.

Do it. Just do it. Ask her out. This night has a purpose. Make it happen.

"The bar here has—"

"There you are," a man in a suit I don't need to see the tag to know cost more than I spent on a down payment to my condo last year walks up and puts his hand on Alice's back.

"Hi," she greets him and then gives me a forced smile.

The man leans in to kiss her cheek. "Did you see enough?" he asks.

"I think so, yes," Alice answers in a tone that I can only describe as emotionless.

"Good. Let's go. The boys want to get an early tee time tomorrow."

"But we—"

"I'll be done in time."

Alice smiles and nods. "Of course."

There it is again. That rehearsed tone.

She turns to face me. The spark I'd seen moments ago in her eyes is gone. "It was a pleasure to meet you, Graham. Enjoy your evening."

What a dick. He didn't even acknowledge that I was here. If she were mine, I'd make sure every man around her knew it.

Alice walks away, suit guy's hand at the small of her back.

Great. Sure. Of course. The first woman I meet in over a

year that I have even a slight urge to ask out turns out to be taken.

That would be my luck.

May as well not press it anymore.

With a shake of my head, I sneak out of the reception.

A bonus of staying at Lovers Lodge, the best lake resort in Wyoming, known for the elegant weddings they put on for the rich and the famous, is their menu. It's twenty-four hours and never disappoints. From the moment Zane mentioned coming here this weekend for the proposal, I've been craving a famous Lodge cheeseburger.

I head for check-in, place a quick order for a burger and fries, and grab a drink at the bar while I wait.

My friends have already left. Go figure.

As soon as my order is up, I down my gin and tonic and head for the elevators.

But I can't wait till I'm in my room. I need the comfort of something normal now. I take the burger from the box and take one bite. The pure exquisite taste of a perfectly grilled burger with two perfect slices of cheese and just enough sauce to give it flavor but not drip down your chin consumes me enough to block out the screaming next to me. I step inside the elevator, hit the button for my floor, and lean back to take another bite.

It's perfect.

That is, until my burger is ripped from my hand. I barely process what's happening before I see it fly past the doors back into the lobby.

"Do not follow me!"

And that's that. My food shatters across fancy suit guy's

face, a pickle landing on his white shirt as the bun hits the floor.

Then the doors close.

I turn to look at the woman next to me.

Alice.

This is not the same woman who shared a quiet corner with me at a reception neither of us were invited to. This version of her is breathing hard and fuming.

I look down at my now-empty hand and then back to the doors.

We ascend, and all I can think is, *what the fuck just happened?*

CHAPTER TWO
PAIGE

Licking ketchup off my palm in an elevator with a man I barely know isn't exactly how I saw my night going.

Grabbing a stranger's food from his hand and tossing it in my fiancé's face is *also* not how I saw this night panning out.

Oh god.

What did I just do?

My mother, father, and Vincent are going to be furious when they find me. I've never been more thankful to not have my phone with me than I am right now.

I put my hand on my stomach and take a breath.

I can't go back to my room. No. Not a chance in hell. Not until I know Vincent has had time to shower and change and breathe. He's not an abusive man, but people saw what just happened, and reputation means everything to Vincent Vellmont. In the world I grew up in, appearance is more important than someone asking me why I tossed a stranger's dinner at the man I'm supposed to marry. No one cares why I did it. All they probably think right now is *oh, poor Paige King has lost her mind. Her family must be devastated. What does this mean for the happy couple?* Not *what did he do? She wouldn't do that for no reason. Is she okay?*

Never, ever, do they ask if she's okay.

I take another breath and lean against the elevator wall, my head back and my eyes closed.

What the heck am I going to do now?

"Um," Graham says next to me. "I was eating that."

I slowly turn my head to look at him, a smile sneaking onto my lips at a time I didn't think was possible.

A time when your fiancé has decided he wants to clear the air from his bachelor party two weeks ago, and from his birthday two months ago, and from my brother's birthday last fall, and so on.

You get it.

Sex. He was having lots of sex. Not with me, of course.

They meant nothing.

They weren't even that good.

Half of them couldn't even bring me to climax.

I gag.

Climax.

Yeah, he said that.

"Oh, I get it. My food grosses you out, so you tossed it out. Well, I'm not sure where you come from, but that's not how that usually works. Also, burgers and fries are just as healthy as any other food if you eat them in moderation, of course."

Instead of answering, I burst into laughter.

"Oh-kay." Graham says and steps away from me. The doors ding, and he bolts, ready to end all communication with me.

Without thinking twice, I follow him.

"Can I hang out with you?" I ask. The words leave my lips as quickly as they came to mind.

He turns around slowly, his eyes wide.

"Let me come in your room with you, and I'll order you another burger. On me. Or well, maybe later on me. I just want to be invisible for a moment, and if I tell someone which room to bill, then people will know where to find me, and the whole point of coming with you is to not be found. Yeah. That's what I want."

I blow out a breath and grin.

Graham leans against the hallway wall, crosses one ankle over the other, and pops a French fry into his mouth.

"Who are these people that you don't want to find you?"

I shrug.

"People."

"The guy who's now wearing my dinner?"

My face wrinkles, and I tap my nose with my index finger.

"Alice, right?"

I nod, slowly. I hate lying. But from the moment Graham looked at me in the ballroom, I knew he didn't know who I was, and for a fleeting moment, I wanted to be anyone but me. Anyone but Paige King. Socialite daughter of Archie King, CEO and owner of three baseball teams, Vans Publishing House, and King Groceries. The largest grocery store chain in all the US. I've been in more magazines than I can count, and bodyguards attend family events as if they were blood related. With the exception of tonight, of course. To my family, I was spending a quiet evening in the resort restaurant with my fiancé, undetected by any paparazzi thus far.

I'm not stupid. I know they're here with their cameras,

ready to capture any moment they can. To be the first to gossip about this weekend. For all I know, someone caught the incident downstairs. At the same time, they might all be hiding tonight. Staying out of trouble if it could cost them the big bucks tomorrow.

"Yes, Alice," I finally answer and point down the hall. "Is your room this way?"

He nods, so I march right past him, ignoring the woodsy scent that surrounds me just like it did in the corner of the reception downstairs.

I'm used to mint and bleach scents that stink of money and what people think are nice smells. Expensive scents are gross. I would know. My mother buys me one every single year for my birthday, and every year, I pawn it and donate the money to one of many foundations.

"You do realize that following me and asking to come into my room is a bit forward. Almost like you have an ulterior motive."

Smiling, I toss my head back a little with a laugh and roll my eyes.

"Trust me. I do not."

"All right, so tell me why you don't want these so-called people to find you."

I bite my lip and nod.

"I just threw a burger in a man's face, Graham. People," I say slowly and make air quotes with my fingers, "are not going to be happy with me. I need to lay low."

"Who says hiding out with me is the right choice? I could be famous."

"Are you?" I ask.

"Nope." He chuckles. "But you didn't know that."

He pushes off the wall and points to the door across from him. "But people," he mimics me, finger quotes and all, "would be very sad if you murder me, so let's not do that."

I snap my fingers. "There go my evening plans."

His door is just ajar as the elevator dings. I shove him inside, tumbling in after. Then the door closes with both of us in a pile on the floor. His fries scatter across the carpet.

I point at him. "Burger *and* fries coming right up."

"So you really didn't know the couple downstairs who got married?"

Graham dips three fries into the honey mustard on his plate before popping them in his mouth and then shakes his head.

"Not a clue."

"Well, I need the story, naturally," I say, reaching over to get a little dressing dip for myself.

"I can't tell you." He smirks.

"Why not?"

"I'm here with my friends. Earlier today, one of my good buddies got engaged. The rest of the evening is a secret."

"Ah." I take a bite of my burger, the one Graham insisted I get. I'll be honest, it's probably one of the best burgers I've ever had. Which is crazy since I've been coming to Lovers Lodge since I was ten. Not once have I ever had a burger when I stayed here. And the fries are so perfectly crunchy, I'll probably dream about them tonight. All I really want to do is devour this entire meal like a starved animal, but I'm also enjoying my conversation with Graham. It's easy. Natural.

It might be menial stuff, but this moment is the most relaxed I've been all weekend, and I'm very invested in knowing why he snuck into the reception of a couple he does not know.

"Secrets are no fun," I say, mouth full before I can stop myself.

I gasp and cover my face with both hands until I'm done chewing.

"That was absolutely inappropriate. I'm so sorry."

I know I'm beet red because my internal body temperature just increased.

I slowly look up at my dinner partner, ready to keep apologizing for my rudeness, when Graham takes a huge bite. "Happens to the best of us," he says, flashing me the food in his mouth.

I laugh, and so does he.

He finishes eating and swallows. "We can call it even now."

"And promise to never do that again."

"It's a deal."

I nod. A comfortable silence falls over us. I've been here for almost an hour now and there haven't been any alerts of any kind that someone is looking for me. My guess is that Vincent knows he'd have to tell my family why I ran off without him, so in order to save face, he hasn't told anyone I'm gone.

"Can I ask you something?" Graham asks, leaning back in his chair.

Gosh, does this man ever stop smiling? Don't get me wrong. I love his smile, but it … it does things to me it shouldn't. It makes me think I'm living a life that isn't mine. But maybe there's a life out there waiting for me.

Jesus, Paige. It's a smile. Calm down.

"As long as it's not why I was at the reception, go for it," I finally answer, preparing myself for a personal question. Outside of how we met, we haven't approached the topic of his first burger, yet I feel it's inevitable the longer we hang out.

"Do you ever relax?" he asks without missing a beat.

Oh.

"What do you mean?"

He points at me with the straw from his Pepsi. "The way you're sitting at this table right now. You look like someone glued a board to your back."

"I can have good posture and be relaxed."

He watches me for a moment, and as much as I want to look away, I can't. His gaze captivates me. My heart starts to beat a little faster under his stare and there's a nervous flutter in my stomach.

I want to know what he's thinking, but asking would just be self-inflicted torture. When this night is over, I'll never see him again.

He grabs his burger and then moves from the small table in his room that we've been sharing to the couch.

He leans back and turns on the TV.

"What are you doing?" I ask.

He grins at me. "Showing you what relaxing looks like."

I roll my eyes and then look out the window.

The moon has placed a mesmerizing glow over Lovers Lake. Anytime I've come here, we get a villa on the lake, so this view from four floors up in the main building isn't one I'm used to seeing.

It's much better than the one I know. This one is calming.

"I am relaxed."

"You're in a hotel room with a stranger, Alice. Are you really?"

I shrug.

Honestly, yes. Like I said, I'm more relaxed around Graham than I have ever been with Vincent. I'm not sure how to process that.

I'm not sure I want to.

"Come. Sit," he says and pats the cushion next to him. "Bring your food."

I look around the room. "I don't see any dinner tray tables."

Another lopsided grin touches Graham's lips. "Yeah, just hold it in your hand."

Without making a show of it or informing him how messy this could get; I do as he says.

"Now, sit."

And I do. I cross one leg over the other and hold my burger in front of me.

He twists to face me, his free hand touching my knee and sending a spark to my already fluttering stomach. It doesn't matter that the fabric of my skirt is between us. He's touching me. That's all my mind can focus on at this point.

Not once, not ever, did I have this reaction to Vincent.

"Okay, just one more thing and then I swear I'll drop it," he says.

"Drop what? Your burger? You're wearing a very nice shirt. I don't recommend doing that."

He chuckles. "If you were alone right now, how would you sit on this couch?"

"You know, I really am—"

"How would you sit, Alice?"

With another eye roll, because every time he says that fake name, guilt washes over me, I push myself back and then crisscross applesauce my legs. Both hands resting in my lap, one of course, still holding my second dinner.

The smile that hits Graham's lips makes me take a quick breath.

How does he do that? Who is this guy?

"Good. Yes," he says and then leans back too.

We're sitting so close that one of my knees rests against his thigh.

My heart pounds from his nearness, and my hands itch to reach for him, but because I know that's absolutely crazy, I take a giant bite of my burger instead and lean back even more.

Who would have thought that sitting on a couch with a burger in my hand and a stranger next to me was going to be the highlight of this weekend?

Not me.

We sit in silence long enough to finish our dinner. Graham cuts the silence by clearing his throat, and don't ask me how I know, but he's about to ask me about Vincent.

"That guy downstairs, who is he to you?"

I let out a breath. "Honestly?"

"Yeah."

He turns his entire body to me, his movement hiking my skirt up to show just the smallest amount of skin. I watch as his gaze drops to it, his hand hovering over the exposed spot before he pulls it back, rubbing the back of his neck as he waits for my answer.

"I'm not sure anymore," is all I can come up with.

"Do you want to talk about this?"

"No."

"Okay."

"But you want to know about him?"

"I want to know that I can check out in the morning and not get my ass kicked for having you in my room."

I laugh. "You won't. Trust me. Vincent isn't leaving his room unless he has to after I tossed a burger in his face."

I assumed my remark was funny, but Graham isn't laughing.

"Vincent," he says and looks at me again. "He has a name." Then he sighs. "Another movie?"

"Yes. Please."

He flips through the channels, finding some action movie that I've already forgotten the name of. He doesn't ask me about Vincent again. In fact, he doesn't talk again until the movie is over, and he excuses himself for the restroom.

I know my time here is limited. It's getting late. I should go, but I really don't want to. Even in silence, having Graham near me is comforting. How is this possible? I don't even know him. It's like I'm in my very own romance novel. It's the scene where when you know, you know.

"Are you sure no one is waiting for you?" Graham asks, stepping out of the bathroom. He yawns and then reaches behind him, jerking his shirt up and over his head.

Holy shit. Okay, don't … *don't what?*

Don't stare!

"Sorry, that was a reflex."

I press a tight smile for him. If I give a real one, he'll know my thoughts.

"It's fine, and yeah, lots of people are waiting for me. I just don't want to go back."

He nods and then rubs his neck again.

"But if you're tired and want to go to bed, I will go."

I head for the door, but he moves quickly. His hand jerks out, his palm rests flat on my stomach as he stops me.

"I … you can stay if you want."

My gaze meets his, and he looks away quickly, shaking his head.

"Hell, what am I saying? Of course you can't stay. You don't know me. I don't know you. This whole night has been …"

"Nice," I answer before he can finish that thought. "Is it weird that I've had a good time? Like, I feel like I've known you for much longer than dinner and a movie or two."

He rubs his chin and studies me. "No. I've enjoyed it too."

"Great. Should we watch another movie?" I suggest. He nods. "Perfect. Just put your shirt back on first."

"Oh, shit, right, sorry."

"It's okay."

We settle back onto the couch with a movie.

Spending my evening with another man is not how I planned to spend the night before my wedding.

CHAPTER THREE
GRAHAM

Having a woman who is clearly attached to another man alone in my hotel room isn't right. Yet, there's something about Alice. I didn't want her to go. I wanted to break the rules for her. I wanted her to need me for as long as she wanted. Hell, I've never slept well when there was another person in my bed. It's a huge reason I've never been in a committed relationship. But last night, with Alice, everything felt different.

It was like I could finally breathe.

Then, I woke up, and she was gone.

It's probably for the best. Luck like that isn't a common thing in the life I live. I've never won a single thing in my life. I've never magically released a bestseller. I've never fallen into an opportunity and had it come out on the winning end. Nope. Everything in my life takes work. A lot of it. Why would finding a woman to spend my life with be any different?

I shower quickly, shaking all thoughts of Alice from my mind, and pack my bag. I'll never see her again, I'm sure of that. Last night was a moment that is now just a memory. Hell, maybe I'll put it in a book.

Actually, that's not a bad idea. I head down to the lobby and to the receptionist's desk. I wasn't going to write this morning until I was back in Wind Valley, but staying a couple hours to get this down while it's fresh is smart. While the environment surrounds me and keeps me in the moment. It is in no way me finding an excuse to possibly run into Alice again.

"Good morning, sir. How can I help you?"

I set my key card on the counter and slide it toward the young woman whose name tag reads Alice. I almost laugh at the coincidence.

"I'm checking out, but I'd like to use your business room for the next hour or two before I have my car pulled around. Can I leave my bag here?"

"Of course. Just tell me your room number, and I'll get it set aside and an order for your car at the time you request."

I provide her the details, catching sight of the crowd in the large lobby.

"Another big event today?" I ask as I wait for her to confirm my car pickup and get me a key for the business room.

"One of our biggest yet. It's Paige King's wedding."

I squint and try to recall the name.

"The daughter of Archie King."

"Ah."

I don't think I've ever heard much about his daughter, but I've read enough about Archie to know what a powerful man he is on his own. Not only does he own King Groceries, the largest grocery store chain in America, but he owns three baseball teams and Vans Publishing House. Vans is the number one publishing house in the country, and I've been trying to get them to notice my books for years. Their connections to foreign rights are incredible, but their connections to movie productions are even better. I want to be one of their authors more than anything. It's the perfect next move for my writing career.

That said, I have no doubt his daughter's wedding is one of the biggest of the year. I'm sure there will be reporters and media of all kinds here today to catch the big moment. I'd stick around to find Archie myself, but from the looks of the lobby, security is strong.

"Yeah, she's marrying a Vellmont."

Again, her eyes light up, but nothing registers to me.

She clears her throat and hands me a card. "Your car will be ready at 10:30 a.m. as requested, and here is the card to the business room. Just return it when you pick up your car."

"Thank you."

I leave my suitcase and sling my computer bag over my shoulder, heading down the hall.

As soon as I'm set up, I spot an email from my agent, Doug. I've been fully self-published since day one. After my twenty-sixth book was released, Doug reached out to me with the idea of selling my backlist to a publisher. Not just any publisher either—we want one of the top five. As I stated, Vans is my number one pick.

I scan the email, taking note that he's reached out to all of them again, but no takers yet. I reply with a fast thank-you and close out of the internet tab.

What if all five houses reject me? I'm not sure what comes next for an indie who has worked his ass off to sell the number of books I do. The money is great, sure, but I don't have awards lining my shelves or publishers fighting over my next release. Do I need a publishing house to keep going? No, not really. But the idea of publishers in a bidding war on a new series of mine because my writing is mesmerizingly addicting would be amazing. Or having my latest cover on a billboard in Times Square because I set a record. Or my name splashed across media site after media site because readers can't put my books down. These are things I didn't know I wanted until Doug sent out emails. And the lack of replies has made me see how badly I want them. Not to mention the movies deals Vans could get me. Put all those things together and that's when I'll know I've made it.

A loud cheer of ladies outside the room pulls my attention. The bridal party no doubt.

I put on my noise-canceling headphones and open a blank word document. I never write scenes in order. I write them as they come to me. I write each in its own document too. As if each scene is its own story, which, technically, it should be to move a story along. I'm not sure which book this scene will go in yet, but I need to get the words down fast.

I start with a man going to the reception of a couple he doesn't know, and my mind drifts to Alice.

I let out a small chuckle. She was so prim and proper eating her burger last night. Hell, I have no doubt she's staying here to be an attendee at this wedding. Vincent. Fuck, when she told me his name, it stung. Like, not actually knowing this guy's name meant I had a chance. Which I knew was crazy, but I thought it anyway.

Still, maybe I'll get lucky and catch one more glimpse of her before I leave. Until then, this scene is my focus.

I spend the next two hours writing my heart out.

I'm a sweet romance writer through and through, but this book is giving me steamy vibes.

When I started back in college, I was nervous to write something with more heat. Then I went down a rabbit hole of staying in my lane. I'd already published an entire series of sweet books and my following was growing, so I just stuck to it and kept building off that sweet brand.

But … it might not be a bad idea to add some spice to my backlist. Steamy is in, and I'm open to the idea. Perhaps being an author who writes both will make me more appealing to publishers.

I nod as if I'm having a conversation with someone.

I'll knock out a steamy book over the next few weeks and send it to Doug when it's done.

Once I'm happy with the words I put down, I head back to the lobby. Partitions line one side of it now with do not enter or private signs hung on them.

"There you are," Zane says and nods at the chaos. "Crazy, isn't it?"

"I'll say. Maybe I should have started a resort like this instead of writing."

"Pssht," he says and nudges my shoulder. "You have the best skill of all of us. Don't forget it."

I roll my eyes. I'm the only sweet romance writer of the group, so I think it's safe to say our writing is currently on two different levels.

"Should we linger to see if we can catch a glimpse of the bride?" Willa says with a giant smile on her face as she looks at her left hand. Her ring shines off the lobby chandelier.

"I will if that's what you want," Zane says, pulling her to his side and kissing her forehead.

"I just heard the receptionist tell someone that she'll be passing through the lobby soon for pictures, so let's give it a chance."

"You got it." Zane kisses her forehead again.

Pictures at 10:30 in the morning—who does that?

"You two have fun playing paparazzi. I'm going to head out."

"Boo, you're no fun."

I playfully nudge Willa with my shoulders as I pass her. Hero, Nora, Beck, and Calla all come into view, stopping me.

"Might want to wait a moment. Guests for this wedding are showing up, and the valet is jammed."

I sigh and turn back around. What kind of people get married this early in the day?

"Guess we can settle in for a bride watch," I say, and Willa squeals.

Hell, maybe if I'm lucky, I'll get that one last glance of Alice.

CHAPTER FOUR
PAIGE

I can't stop smiling.

A giddy feeling takes over and I giggle. I actually giggle.

"Yes, oh yay!" my cousin, Paisley, says behind me as she adjusts my veil.

"I'm so happy to see you smiling, Paige. You had me worried for a moment that maybe you didn't want to marry Vincent today."

My smile drops.

Oh, right. Vincent.

I'd been so mentally wrapped in thoughts of how I stayed up way too late last night talking to a man who I can't stop thinking about. About how I woke up in bed with another man. Who cares if we were on top of the covers? I'd never felt so at peace before.

But, of course, I glanced at the clock, and the fairy tale I'd been in had to end.

I force a smile. It's flat, but I don't think she notices that it's not real. There are only two people in my family who have ever called me out for my fake smile: my father and my brother, Preston. Neither are in this room right now.

If Preston were here, he'd call me out so fast and have me in a car headed far, far away. He's never liked Vincent.

But I am a King, and Kings have a reputation. So, I hold my faux smile as long as I can.

"It's my wedding day," I say. That's it. I won't elaborate. Anyone listening can take that statement however they want.

I inhale and run my hand over the dress's lace.

It's beautiful. Of course it is. It was made for me, and it was made exactly how I wanted. You know, after my mother and soon-to-be mother-in-law picked a designer for me.

The door to the room bursts open, and as if her ears were burning, my mother glides in.

Now, it's really showtime. My mother has been awaiting this day longer than anyone I know. Well, she and Vincent's mother. They are basically the only reason we're getting married. We were groomed to be together since the day we were born. Okay, that's a little harsh. Vincent, despite his recent admissions, wasn't always a douchebag. The start of our relationship was real, or it was to me. Then, when the mention of our families merging in both business and family was mentioned at a dinner event one evening, he proposed less than a month later. I'm not sure if any of this has ever been real to him or if he's just playing the role.

Wait. Wait. That's right. After last night, I officially know that answer.

"Oh, dear," my mother coos and presses her palms together. "You are breathtaking."

"Thank you, Mom."

She lets out a huge sigh. "You know, I just checked the reception, and the turnout is spectacular. This wedding will be talked about for years, Paige, dear. Years."

I force a smile.

"Oh, and did I mention that the same musician who was available for your proposal is here tonight as well? She was an added surprise. You're welcome."

I tilt my head and open my arms to hug her.

She means well. She wants what's best for me, and in her mind, what's best is having the biggest and best of everything. It also means being talked about for years. Like I said, reputation is big for her and the circle I grew up in.

It's why I'm standing here right now.

It's why I'm about to head downstairs to get my photos taken.

It's why I said yes that morning when Vincent got down on one knee.

Yeah, it was a whole breakfast thing.

He likes mornings. For everything. Hence, why it's so early, and I'm ready for bridal party pictures so that we can have a wedding that begins at noon sharp.

"Thank you. I'm sure the guests will adore her music."

"Of course they will. This will set her up for years of events. I enjoy knowing that I progressed someone else's career today." She turns to leave but stops to perfect the bridesmaids' outfits. One has a strap too loose, another needs her hair re-pinned, and Vincent's sister is complaining about her eye makeup.

I didn't pick my bridesmaids.

That should have been another sign of many for me.

I wanted Grace to be my maid of honor. Grace's family owns Lovers Lodge. Her dad and my dad are old friends from college. Our circles are different, but she's one of the only people I trust in this world. I met her the first summer we came here, and she's been a constant in my life ever since. I could go as far as to call her my best friend.

My mother rejected the idea because, of course, who else would be able to handle the wedding if she weren't working and running the lodge on my big day?

Speaking of the angel, Grace arrives with a big smile. It fades slowly when she sees me, but I don't think anyone noticed but me. Right, she also knows what my real smile looks like.

"Are you good?" she mouths.

I nod, just once.

As soon as I'd left Graham's room this morning, I found her in her office and told her everything. Everything about Vincent and everything about Graham.

She offered to fake a kitchen fire that needed the entire resort to evacuate, but I told her it wasn't necessary. I'm a big girl. I'll marry Vincent and let our families merge for the greater good. As unhappy as I am about it, my family has never treated me poorly or not supported me. I've never wanted for anything in my life, so marrying Vincent doesn't seem like a hardship to thank them.

Wow.

Thinking it now … being here now, I—

"The stage is ready for pictures. I've got the lobby partitioned off and ready for you to head down."

Stage?

"Head down." My mother puts her hand on her chest. "Grace, dear, isn't there another way you could say that?"

"Mom," I say and smile at Grace.

I stay behind with Turner, my family's head of security. Once everyone is ready for me, he leads the way, and we take the elevator down. It's a good thing the girls took my veil, because the amount of tulle from the veil and my dress would not have fit in here. The veil alone is obscene.

"Wait here. I need to secure the floor."

He leaves without waiting for a response from me. I'm not his boss, so even if I objected, he wouldn't listen. I want to ask why, if keeping me hidden till the big reveal is such a big deal, does he trust that no one will see me in the few minutes he needs to complete his task. Hell, my dress is poofy enough to hint there is obviously a bride just on the other side of the dividers.

I don't have the chance to ask, though. He's gone.

I let out a breath.

Marrying Vincent could be worse. He will be good to me and treat me kindly, and in every physical and visual sense, he'll be the perfect husband.

I'll never want for anything, and my family will be proud of me.

Then again, even if I didn't marry him, I'd never want for anything.

A perk, I suppose, of being born into a family that's already wealthy.

Your image is created for you from day one. I never had the choice of what life I wanted—this one was picked for me. Don't get me wrong, I love the foundation work I do, but I'll never know what my life could have been had I been in charge. Had I put myself first. Had I picked out a career for myself. What if I wanted to do marketing? Or even be a vet. I love animals.

God, listen to me, the rich girl about to get married in the resort of her dreams and she's still unhappy.

Talk about cliché, huh?

I mean, it's not like I can have the life I had last ni—

Laughter from somewhere close and movement from the corner of my eyes stops my next thought.

I look so fast that my neck pops, but I ignore the pain as Graham comes into view. He can't see me, of course. That's the way this is planned, but I can see him.

All of him.

The way he's standing with a group of others who I can only assume are the friends he came here for this weekend. The way he laughs at something one of them says. The way lifts his coffee cup to his mouth and sips. He looks in my direction, but like I said, he can't see me.

One of the guys he's with glances at the partitions and nods. Graham shrugs. They both look away.

That's it. That's the last time I'm going to see that man.

My heart physically aches at the thought. Tears prick at my eyes. I've never felt this before. This fear of never seeing someone again.

Graham waves to his group as they head for the guest elevator. But not Graham—he walks for the front door instead, his suitcase rolling behind him as he hands a ticket to the valet in exchange for his keys.

It doesn't take me but a moment to spring into action.

I turn, hike up my dress, and run out the front door before anyone can stop me or notice that I'm gone.

Graham closes his driver's door just as I jerk open the back seat and hop in, stuffing my dress safely inside before closing the door.

"Get me out of here, please," I say. His eyes are round saucers.

All I see is the tick of his jaw before he's pulling away.

Holy shit.

CHAPTER FIVE
GRAHAM

I have no one to blame but myself.

I wanted excitement in my life. I wanted to do things that made me step out of my comfort zone. Crashing a wedding reception is one thing but being the getaway driver for a bride —yeah, that tops the cake.

After my third turn, I clear my throat.

"I…" that's all I say. Hell, I have no idea what to even ask right now. That's saying a lot for a man who uses words every single day of his life.

What the fuck? feels too insensitive to ask. Are you okay? seems predictable. Tell me what's going on is too demanding. Am I going to get charged with kidnapping? That's … reasonable.

I glance in the rearview mirror, but the tear sliding down Alice's cheek stops any words from coming out of my mouth. Instead, I reach into my computer bag and grab a Snickers bar.

I reach toward the back seat to offer it to her and as soon as she looks at it, she smiles.

She also grabs the bar and takes a huge bite.

"Oh god, that's good."

"First Snickers bar?" I ask as a joke.

"In like five years, yes."

I make a choking noise and then meet her gaze in the mirror.

"I—"

"I—" we say at the same time.

"My name isn't Alice," she says quickly with a sigh, finishing off the chocolate bar. "It's Paige."

I nod slowly.

"I sort of gathered that when a ball of white fluff dove into my car."

"I was supposed to get married today," she goes on, grabbing the frill on her dress and tossing a piece into the air. "Obviously."

"Obviously," I repeat.

Silence takes over as we hit the highway.

"Oh shit," I say and start to slow down. "I should have asked where you want to go. I was just driving home, and I didn't think—"

"Home sounds good."

"Yeah." I give a slight chuckle. "I'm sure our homes aren't exactly next door to each other."

"I know that. What I mean is, your home sounds good. Anywhere sounds good. The zoo, a bar, a karaoke club, a jail cell, or shoot, I didn't mean that I'm so desperate that I'd take a jail cell over your house. I just mean—"

"Paige, it's okay. You can come with me."

From the rearview mirror, I watch as she bites her bottom lip, slowly letting it go with a pop.

"Is this weird?" she asks.

"Oh, fuck yeah. Totally. Yes. Craziest thing I've done in all my life."

"Right. I didn't mean to put you in this position. You can drop me off somewhere if you want."

I let out a deep laugh.

There is no way in hell I'm letting her out of my sight until I know she's taken care of and okay.

"Not a chance. Not on the side of some highway. I live a couple of hours away. You can ride with me and then make a plan. How does that sound?"

"Insane." She smiles. "But oddly enough, that idea makes me feel like I can breathe, so I think it's a wonderful plan."

She starts to fidget with her dress.

My focus flashes between her and the road in front of me.

I clear my throat when she clearly can't get the fluff of her dress to cooperate.

"Since our entire relationship is just one weird moment after the next, might I suggest one more?" I ask.

"Yes, please." She folds her hands in her lap as I pull off to the side of the road.

"I have a suitcase in the back with sweats and a T-shirt. They might be more comfortable for the ride. I can grab them, let you change, and then we can get back on our way."

"Deal." Her face lights up. "But let me top your request and ask that you help me get out of this dress. I can't do all the buttons in the back on my own."

Sure. Help undress her. I can do that.

Fuck.

We both get out of the car, and I grab some clothes for her.

"You can change in the back seat if you want," I offer. Changing outside means anyone could see her, and that's not okay with me.

"That sounds great," she says and spins. "I can't seem to get a hold of the little loop thing to do it myself, but maybe if you get it started, I can finish."

As soon as I see the line of buttons—teeny tiny buttons, might I add? I laugh.

"Can you even breathe in this? It's sealed up like Fort Knox."

"Wait till you see what I'm wearing underneath."

I pause my hands over the first button.

"Oh god, I didn't mean it like that. I just meant that … why is this happening to me?"

I get to work before I reply. "I know what you meant. And I think it's because you just ran out on your wedding like a madwoman."

Silence falls between us, and by the time I get to button ten, I open my mouth to apologize, but she beats me to it.

"I don't feel mad. Flustered, a little, but"—she lets out a breath of a laugh— "I'm standing on the side of the road taking my clothes off, and I'm much happier right here than I was the entire morning getting ready for the day."

Again, I'm not sure what to say. She's got a lot to process right now. That, and I've reached the lace corset underneath, which in turn reveals a glimpse of her silky undergarments.

My heart races and my jeans grow tight.

I back up.

She legit just ran out on her wedding, Graham. Pull it together.

"Are you done?" she asks, looking over her shoulder.

I nod. "Yeah. Might have done more than enough. Sorry."

"Don't be. This is wonderful."

I hand her my clothes and walk toward the trunk as she climbs into the back seat. I wait until I hear her step out again before I turn.

"All set?"

Her hands are on his hips as she nods and looks through the car window.

Her dress takes up most of the back.

"Can I sit up front with you?"

I nod, swallowing the lump in my throat. Though they swallow her, she looks damn good wearing my clothes.

"Of course."

We get back in the car and pull back onto the road without a word.

"Graham?"

"Yeah."

"I'm really glad you were at the lodge this weekend."

I set the cruise control and then meet her gaze. She's got her head leaned back on the headrest as she watches me.

For someone who just made a huge life-altering choice in her life, she looks mighty damned relaxed in my passenger seat.

I like knowing I did that for her.

"You know what? So am I."

CHAPTER SIX

PAIGE

It's official.

I'm a runaway bride.

I'd be lying if I say a part of me doesn't feel guilty about what I just did. Don't get me wrong, it was the best choice I've ever made. I feel free, like my head is finally clear after months of wedding planning.

I do feel bad for Grace, who is probably freaking out right now. Hell, I told her about this random man I met last light and then bam, I go missing. Although, it's not exactly that I went missing. I have no doubt at least one person saw me jump in his car of my own free will.

Well, I hope someone did, for Graham's sake.

I should probably ask him to use his phone to at least call Grace. Or my brother. Or my dad. Oh god. My dad. The backlash he's probably getting from my mother right now is probably out of control. I don't have to guess. I know my mother. She's probably demanding to call the FBI or something equally dramatic.

"You've been awfully quiet. Which is understandable, and although I'm a stranger, I have ears. A couple of good ones that would be willing to listen to anything you want to talk about."

I keep my focus out the window to hide my smile.

He's just making a simple statement to tell me he's here for me if I want to talk, but the way he says it, it's like ... like he knows to put a little humor in it because smiling right now is exactly what I need.

I take a breath, hold my head high, and turn to face him. "Are you sure about that? Everything going on in this brain is pretty heavy."

"Lay it on me," he says and then winks.

He freaking winks.

Those flutters from last night return to my stomach. He's winking at a runaway bride. Why does this make me like him even more?

Maybe it's because this man has given me more attention than Vincent ever has, and since I'm not used to it, I'm taking it more personally than I should.

Still, talking things out always helps.

"It's a lot," I say again.

"We still have at least another hour. Maybe talking will make it go by faster."

"Yeah."

"Of course, as we have very well established, you don't know me, and I understand if—"

"He cheated on me," I blurt out.

Graham doesn't say a word, so I chance a glance just in time to see his jaw tick and his hands grow tighter on the steering wheel.

"He told me last night. Hence, the burger in his face."

"He got lucky."

"Ha, sooooooo many times, it seems."

"Oh, I—"

"I know you didn't. But you know what the craziest part is? I got ready today. I did my hair, I did the makeup, I put on the dress. I was still going to marry him."

I let out a huff, trying to gather my thoughts about who I was a little more than an hour ago to the woman I am now. We are two completely different people.

I feel the prick of tears but swallow them down.

"I think I knew I didn't want to marry him the day he proposed, but our families are under constant watch, and that day, there were cameras everywhere. I didn't want to embarrass him." Another huff laugh. "I guess it's clear now that was not an emotion that went both ways."

"He's an idiot, Paige."

"Yeah, but what does that make me? A coward? I couldn't even confront him. I just ran."

"I think it makes you brave and strong for finally taking control of your life."

"Don't do that."

"Do what?"

"Be sweet. I just ruined the lives of so many people."

He shakes his head. "No, you didn't ruin anything. You might have rearranged their day, but they will get over it. And if they love you, they will be happy about the choice you made."

He looks over at me for a brief moment before watching the road again.

It was a quick glance, but enough for me to know he

meant every word and he wasn't just saying it because he thought it was something I wanted to hear.

"Maybe I just ruined my life."

"How so?"

I shrug.

"What am I going to do now? Going back feels like I'd be returning to the wrong place, but if I don't go back to the only life I know, where do I go? What do I do? I don't even know what I want."

The truth of it is, despite everything I just said, there are parts of my life I enjoy. The foundations I run being a big one. I mostly focus on those for children. My first ever best friend, Kendall, died of cancer when we were in the seventh grade, and I knew from that moment on that I wanted to find a way to help kids like her and their families. I just started a new foundation for kids with cancer, too. The first dinner for the event is in a couple of months. Vince and I started it together, and the event was going to be our first appearance as a married couple.

Yay.

"To my place."

"What?"

"You come to my place," he says again so simply.

"Sure, for a night, maybe, but then—"

"Or more than a night," he cuts in. "Look, it's weird for me to offer you a place to live, I get it. Our entire relationship to this point is weird. But asking you to stay with me feels right."

"And what? I'd be your roommate?"

He nods. "I have an extra room and a bathroom that would be all yours. We'd share the living room and kitchen, of course, but you'd have your own space to just be while you figure things out. Take a week, a month, two months, six, whatever you need. I'm actually going to be gone a lot over the next month. It would be like you have your own place."

He's giving me a choice. He's asking me what I want. Not even two hours ago, I was thinking that I was never given this opportunity and now it's being offered to me.

How is that possible?

It all sounds wonderful, but there is always a *but* in situations like this. I'm a King after all. We don't take generous offers like this without having to give something in return. And right now, as much as I want to rush into this and tell him yes, I have nothing to give Graham.

"If I say yes, what do you want from me?"

"What?"

"What do you want in return for letting me stay with you? I have money, yes, but accessing it right now would bring attention to where I am, and I'm not so sure I want that. So I can pay—"

"I don't want your money, Paige. Ever. Let's make that clear now."

"Then what do you want?"

"Nothing. The comfort of knowing you're safe while you decide what you want your next move to be."

I study him for a moment.

Who is this man?

"That's it?"

He nods. "That's it."

Just when I think he's going to add more to his statement or tell me he's joking and that there is actually something he wants from me, he points out the window.

"That's Wind Valley," he says with a smile, and I can tell through his tone that he loves where he lives.

I peek out the window and see the mountain backdrop and the town below it.

"Is it a small town?" I ask.

"It depends on who you ask." He's got one arm on the wheel, his wrist resting at the top while his hand hangs over it and the other arm propped on the center console. "To me, yes, it's small."

"What's the population?"

He chuckles. "That's your follow-up question?"

I smile at his flirty tone and also the way he was able to change the subject so gracefully. "Yes, it is. I like to know these things."

"Ah, okay. Just under ten thousand."

"Sounds small to me too."

"Well, compared to where you live, I'm sure it does."

Silence falls as I replay the action of the day again.

"There you go again. Lost in thought. What are you thinking about?"

His voice pulls me out of the stunned state I was beginning to fall into. I glance at him quickly and then back at my hands. Why does this guy make me want to confess every last detail about my life? I don't know him, and there isn't a single cell in my brain that says I should hide myself. Not a single one.

I wave a hand in front of my face.

"Just more thoughts on this day. You get the gist of it. I don't want to bore you with this topic just because I'm still processing it."

"Paige," he says quietly. "One thing you should know

about me is that if I didn't care, I wouldn't ask. I care about you and your day. I can't even begin to think of the number of emotions you're feeling right now. And I get that you'll be thinking about this today and tomorrow and the day after or longer, but guess what? On each of those days, I will ask you to share your thoughts with me. I will be here for you if you let me."

I've said it before and I'll say it again: who the hell is this guy, and why could we not have met sooner? Years sooner, months, before Vincent. My life and this day could have been so much different if it had been Graham I'd been meeting at the end of the aisle.

I blow out a breath.

"I'm thinking that I always imagined my wedding day would be a bit different."

"Oh really? You didn't plan on running out and jumping into a stranger's car?" He flashes me a grin, and I roll my eyes.

"It was on my mood board and everything."

"I'll bet."

"But seriously, to be honest, I didn't choose any part of this ceremony."

He reaches behind us and holds up part of my dress. "Not even this?"

I shake my head. "It's a beautiful dress. Vera is so good at design, but it's not me."

"Vera." He chuckles. "You say it like you two are on a first-name basis."

"Considering she's one of the guests I just stood up, yeah, we are."

"Are you serious?" His voice rises a little and his brows jump.

I nod.

"Fuck. We really do live different lives."

"We did," I say, "but it looks like I'm your new roommate, so you're stuck with me for now."

"Ah, that's what I wanted to hear."

As we pull into Wind Valley and take turn after turn until we reach his building, I can't help but envy his world. The one he's clearly happy to be back to and feels like he could share with me.

"Should we take your dress upstairs?" he asks as we get out of the car, and he pulls his bags from the trunk.

"Um, not right now. I don't want to draw attention."

He nods. "Right, good point. Mrs. Mason next door is always trying to set me up with her granddaughter. If she saw us heading inside with a wedding dress in tow, she'd make sure the entire building and then some knew of my relationship status update."

I smile. "You know all your neighbors?"

"Not all of them," he says and nods for me to follow. "Maybe like ten of them."

I head for the first door, but Graham moves for the steps. As he ascends, I look up. Each apartment must have outdoor access since I don't see a main building or a doorman or anything to greet him. He just pulls in, gets out, and goes to his place without anyone noticing.

Not a single person knows I'm here.

I can just move around freely.

This is insane.

As if I haven't smiled enough, I do it again, but bigger.

I follow him up the stairs, and he tells me about the neighbors on the first two floors. Parents of his friends or friends of his parents. Each landing has two apartments, which means they share the space in front of their doors. When he reaches the fourth floor, he stops.

"Mrs. Mason lives across from me."

"So, are you the youngest in this building?"

"You caught on to that, huh?"

"I did."

"Well, it's quiet here. I think older people love it, and it's nice for when I need to put my head down and really get to work."

We step inside, and instantly, I gasp. "This was not what I was expecting, Graham. Oh my gosh."

Not that I really had an idea. I just know this wasn't it.

This is not your typical apartment. It's a full-blown condo. The kitchen is huge and opens right up to a modern living space of grays and whites. There's a gorgeous balcony just past the sliding doors. It's covered in greenery and flowers with two chairs and a small table.

It's my exact style and taste, too.

He sets his phone and keys down in the kitchen, so I follow him, my hand gliding over the marble as I prepare to take in what I'll be calling home for who knows how long.

His phone rings.

Both of us flinch at the noise vibrating against the countertop.

"It's the lodge," he says and reaches for it. "Do I answer it?"

I shrug. "Do they have a reason to call you?"

"Yeah." He chuckles and points at me with the phone.

"That place is loaded with cameras, Paige. I'm sure someone got my plate number or something and they know you're with me."

"Well, if they are calling about me, it wouldn't be the lodge."

His head volleys. "Good point."

"Just answer it."

"Hello?" he answers, turning to give me his back. I quickly march around him to watch his reaction to the call.

"Oh, hi, Grace. What can I do for you?"

I let out a breath and stick my hand out, gesturing for him to hand me the phone.

He shakes his head.

"She's my friend. I promise."

Without saying a word, he hands me his cell.

"Hi, Grace."

"Holy shitballs, Paige. What the hell? I mean, I'm so freaking proud of you, but Jesus, a head's up would have been nice, and who is this guy? Graham Wright. Do you know him? Is this the guy from last night? Oh my god. It's just now occurring to me that you ran off on your wedding day with another man."

I sigh and sit on the couch.

"I should have given you a head's up. I am sorry for that, but to be honest, until I jumped in his car, I didn't know I was going to run."

"Are you safe?"

"I am."

I hear her let out a long breath. "Good. If you say you are, then I believe you. How are you doing?"

"I'm okay. Hey, um, does anyone know where I am?"

"Not yet. But they asked me to review the footage from your mad dash. I have like five minutes before I have to go give some sort of update to them."

"They let you review it without my dad's security?"

"Barely. I had to pull the whole 'you're my best friend, and I want to find you just as badly, and I own this place' card. They are not happy."

"Can I ask you a favor?"

"If it's to lie about the footage, I don't think I can."

"Please, Grace. Please."

"Paige, your dad will know I'm lying, and then he will have people out searching for you. It could get ugly fast."

"Please, Grace. Make something up. Or just pull my dad aside and tell him you spoke with me, and I'm fine."

"Ugh, fine. But you better call or text me every single day. How am I even going to get a hold of you?"

"This number for now, I guess." Graham is watching me. He nods. "But don't give it to anyone else. I'll keep in touch, I promise."

"I love you, Paige."

"I love you too."

I hang up and hand Graham back his phone.

"Now what?" I ask, clasping my hands together and standing.

"Now, I'll show you your room and then we'll go get you some things to live here."

"I don't have any money, Graham."

"I'm aware, Paige," he says over his shoulder. "I don't care."

"I don't want anyone to know I'm here."

"So then we order off Amazon, and you wear my clothes and use my things for a couple of days."

"Are you going to have an answer for everything I say?"

"Yes. Now, follow me."

I do, because I may not have any clue as to what's going on in my life, but I do know this: I trust Graham. I feel safe here when he's near me.

I don't want that feeling to end.

CHAPTER SEVEN
GRAHAM

I'm about two thousand more words into my current work in progress by the time Paige comes into the kitchen the next morning in nothing but my T-shirt. It's solid black, but I know with one quick glance that she's not wearing the shorts I gave her. Her hair, which was pinned up all day yesterday and the night before that, now falls free around her face and over her shoulders. She pauses in the doorway, tugging at the shirt.

"Oh, I didn't think you would be awake yet."

I glance at the time on my computer. "It's 8:00 a.m."

"And?"

"And normally by this time, I've gone for a run, cooked breakfast, and finished my morning word count."

"Your morning word count?"

I nod. I couldn't sleep last night, and during the time I spent staring at my ceiling fan, it crossed my mind how much Paige and I do not know about each other. Yes, we mentioned that small fact more than once yesterday on the drive here, but even when we said it, we never bothered to fix it. The fact that we both felt comfortable while knowing next to nothing about the other speaks volumes. I just don't know how to process it. So, today I plan to get to know her better. I'm going to ask questions to see how I can help her while she's here.

"Care to elaborate on what word count means?"

I click save and lean back.

"I'm a writer, and I like to publish three to four books a year, which means that my word count needs to be consistent every day."

"Seriously?" Her face beams. "What kind of writer? Is that what you were doing last night while I was watching TV?"

"It was. I try to write every morning and night."

She slinks into the seat across from me.

"So, my watching TV didn't bother you. I'm sorry I went … silent toward the end of the day. Especially after everything you've done for me."

I could remind her of what I told her yesterday in the car about her being able to talk to me about anything, but I won't. She knows where I stand, and I'm learning that she feels the need to apologize when she doesn't do what she thinks someone expects of her. I want her to be comfortable here. I want her to get the peace she's clearly seeking from her current life. I want to be a safe space for her.

So, yeah, last night after she told me she didn't want to go out to get clothes and other things because she didn't want anyone to see her, we placed an order on Amazon. Then, after she showered and put on a new pair of my shorts and a shirt, she sat quietly in the living room watching TV. Did it bother me? Not one bit. I still got my writing in, and she seemed content to sit there without me.

That said, I may or may not have written a scene where the heroine was wearing the hero's clothes, and the hero was imagining all the ways he could remove those clothes because of what they did to him.

I am a man, after all, and despite our circumstances, the fact that I'm attracted to Paige is not a secret.

"What kind of books do you write?" she asks.

"Romance."

"Wow. The confidence when you said that was hot."

I clear my throat, and she shakes her head. "Sorry."

"Don't be sorry," I tell her. "I'm confident in what I write."

"Good. What kind of romance do you write?"

Considering she's been extremely open with me about her life, I choose to do that same.

"Sweet novels."

"Huh. I was expecting something like a thriller, but sweet sounds like my kind of romance novel."

"You read a lot?"

I can picture it. She'd be sitting in some big fancy white fluffy chair with her legs tucked under while she holds a book. She looks more like a paperback kind of woman.

"I used to. Oddly enough, my family owns a publishing company, but if you write romance novels for a living, I'm sure you knew that."

I nod. "It did occur to me."

She watches me closely, as if she's waiting for me to say more.

Do I want to ask her if she has tips or something to help me get in with Vans? Sure. But it doesn't feel right.

She shrugs as if she doesn't know what else to say about it.

"Anyway, you said you usually run in the morning. I hope I didn't keep you from it today. I actually like to run too. Maybe once I have more clothes and some decent shoes, you can wake me up to go with you."

"We could go get some today if you want."

Her nose wrinkles, and she shrugs again.

"Or I can go get them if you remind me of your size."

"Thank you. I'm still not sure I want anyone to know where I am just yet."

"Won't people be looking for you?"

"I think Grace might have helped with that. Time will tell."

Paige rises then and opens two cupboards before she finds the mugs and pours herself some coffee. I pull my eyes away from where the hem of my shirt meets her slender thighs and turn my computer just slightly so I can get back to it. I need a distraction. I write about all those "when you know, you know" moments, but I've never actually lived it. I'm not saying that's what's happening here, but damn, I have no idea what to call it.

She ran out of her own wedding yesterday and is standing in my kitchen, and honestly, I've never felt this happy. And yet, that single fact right there is why no matter how my brain or body reacts to her, nothing can come of it. I'm ready to find the one, and she's a runaway bride. How much more opposite can we get?

"So what do you do during the day when you aren't writing?" she asks. My gaze shouldn't be focused on the way her lips touch the mug, but they are.

I fidget in my seat.

"It depends. I find things here and there. I go on hikes or

do something active. For the next few months, however, I've got book signings to attend and family to see."

"They don't all live here?"

"I have one sister in Denver, one in Texas, and one in Nashville."

"Oh wow, three sisters."

"Three sisters, three brothers-in-laws, and too many nieces and nephews to count."

Her nose wrinkles. "That's cute. You're a family guy. I like that."

"I try. Our parents were older when they had me. I'm the youngest, so they're all I have. Family and books about sums me up."

"I highly doubt that."

"What do you do?" I ask. It's such a basic question, but honestly, how else do you ask it?

"I manage different foundations or anything else they need from me." She sighs and sits in the seat next to me. Her knees bump mine. "I actually just started a new foundation for kids with cancer. The first fundraiser dinner is in a couple months." She takes another sip. "It was going to be the first public appearance Vincent and I made as a married couple. It made sense since we started it together."

"Damn," I say and then clear my throat. I hadn't meant to say that out loud.

"Tell me about it."

She rises with her mug and walks into the living room.

"Hey," I call out, "can I ask you something?"

"Mm-hmm," is her answer as she browses my book-shelves.

"This is in no way me wanting you to leave, but why do you think you can't go home?"

Her mouth twists, and she nods at my computer.

"I can go home. But I mostly want to avoid the media. I can only imagine what they're saying. And my mother will, without a doubt, be furious with me. She means well, but she was looking forward to this more than anyone."

I'm listening to her, but I click on the web browser at the same time.

"And what do you want to accomplish while you're here?"

Instead of answering, she lets out a laugh. "Boy, aren't you full of questions this morning?"

Heat creeps up my neck. "I'm sorry. I'm not really a beat around the bush kind of guy if I can help it."

"It's okay. Honestly, right now, I just want to not have a plan. I want to not have to do anything but just … be here. Drinking this coffee and wearing only a shirt."

"Got it."

Paige hasn't said more about her mad dash yesterday, but fuck, does the media have their opinions. The only thing I'm grateful for is the lack of photos of me or my 4Runner. It's solid black, and there's a photo of her reaching for the handle, but that's it. Honestly, I think it all happened so quickly that people couldn't process it. *Paige King Secretly Married Another. King Heiress Misses Wedding to Attend Rehab. The Daughter of Archie King Too Drunk to Attend Her Own Wedding. Runaway Bride Paige King Is MIA.*

Jesus. Minus that last one, where the hell are these people getting their information? I knew I never believed the tabloids before, but this is just more confirmation of why I hate social media of all kinds. If it weren't for my books, I wouldn't be on it.

I glance at the woman who is now moving around in my kitchen and helping herself to everything as if she belongs here. I push down how much I enjoy seeing her here.

Three days if you include today. That was it. That was it for me to develop feelings for her.

But it doesn't matter.

Her entire life just shifted. She told me flat out she doesn't know what to do from here, and I'm not about to be another thing she has to worry about.

I clear my throat. If anything, though, she does need someone who isn't going to lie or treat her like glass. She proved that yesterday.

"Since we are sort of on the topic of the media, I let curiosity get the best of me this morning, and I looked online about yesterday."

"Oh," she says and then sighs as if this happens to her all the time. "How bad is it?"

I volley my head and twist my lips. "No one thinks you've been kidnapped, so I think we're in the clear on that aspect. Nor are there pictures of my car, so I think you can safely hide away here until you're ready to go back, but I'm afraid most of the world might be under the impression that you have a drug problem."

She stares blankly at her coffee and nods slowly. The emotionless expression on her face makes me feel uneasy.

"Okay, what are your plans today?" she says, snapping out of whatever trance she was in as she looks up at me.

"That's it?"

Surely, she has more to say about the subject. Or questions

even. Maybe. I don't know. Something more than asking me about *my* plans. I shouldn't be on her mind at this time.

"I can't do anything about it, Graham. Whatever you're looking at is already printed. I can only control how I react. I know they're all wrong. So yeah, what are your plans today? I don't imagine you're going to cancel everything to stay here with me."

I try not to grin. Now, I know I've never judged her or thought of her as some princess who thinks it's her way or no way, but honestly, she's probably the most down-to-earth billionaire out there. I have so many follow-up questions, but maybe I've asked enough for today. She's clearly avoiding things, so I should respect that and let her. If she wants to move on to a new topic, that's what we will do.

"I'm meeting my friends this morning for a writing session."

When Simon first suggested meeting on Monday, getting a head start on writing for the week sounded great since I'll be hitting the road in a couple days. Obviously, now I wish I hadn't agreed.

"I can cancel."

"Oh my gosh, please don't do that. Don't change anything for me. Do you have more friends who write?"

I nod.

"Here in Wind Valley?"

I nod again.

"I love that."

I start to pack up my bag and then pause.

"We usually meet for a few hours. I should be back by lunch. Are you going to be okay alone?" I ask, hesitating in the doorway.

She nods and lets out a small laugh. "Honestly, I'm looking forward to it."

"Oh yeah, sick of me already, huh?"

"Not even a little."

She follows me to the door.

"What if you need something? I should get you a phone while I'm out."

Her eyes go wide. "Please don't."

"Why not?"

"You've already spent enough money on me, Graham."

"So?"

"So, I don't want you spending anymore. Plus, I like being unreachable right now. It's nice that you're the only person who knows where I am."

"And Grace," I add.

"Oh, yes."

"Maybe I should get you a phone for her, at least. To stay in contact."

She shakes her head. "Not happening."

I open my mouth to say more, but instead I hold up my pointer finger, set my bag down, and jog to my room and back.

I hold my iPad up in her face.

"If I add to the notes on my phone, it'll pop up here. If you add to it, same thing."

"It's really going to bother you that you can't contact me, isn't it?"

I shrug. "It would make me feel better, yes."

She holds eye contact with me, neither of us looking away in challenge. Finally, she groans. "Fine. But I'm not going to need anything. Is there a password?"

Oh hell.

"Graham writes romance pound one. All one word."

"Cute." She winks at me.

"Okay." But I don't move. "Are you sure you're going to be okay alone right now?"

She pushes me out the door. "Yes. Go. Now. Go see your friends."

I lift my bag over my shoulder once more and study her carefully.

"I'm not sure how I feel about leaving you in my apartment alone."

She rolls her eyes, crosses her arms, and leans against the doorframe. Her gaze bounces like a pinball ball at my stance, which in turn causes me to rub the back of my neck.

"I'm not going to steal anything."

"That's not what I'm worried about."

"Oh." She smiles. "You're worried someone will find me and finally think you kidnapped me, huh?"

"I'm worried that you won't get the chance to find out who you are or what you want out of staying here before they find you."

Well, shit. Yep, I said that out loud.

The flirty smile she'd been dawning fades, but she quickly recovers by engulfing me in a hug. When it's clear she isn't letting go, I wrap my arms around her and hold on tight.

My heart races at having her in my arms, and my mind tells me once more not to let this one go.

But all too soon, she's stepping back. With her hands resting on my hips, she says, "I'll be here when you get back. Have fun."

I close the door before I do something crazy like kiss her goodbye.

Because I'll be honest: after just a couple days with her, I've never wanted to kiss someone so badly in my entire life.

The list of reasons why that can't happen is longer than I care to admit.

No matter my feelings, the reality is, she won't be here forever. My place is just a stopping point for her. A place for her to regroup before she goes back to a life that is nothing like the one I have here.

CHAPTER EIGHT
PAIGE

I told myself that I wouldn't snoop. This man who doesn't know anything about me, the real me, is kind enough to help me—going through his apartment isn't the nice thing to do.

At the same time, although I'm still alive and well, I should get to know him a little more. I could sense that was his plan this morning but asking him questions about himself meant that he'd ask questions about me, and outside of loving my newest foundation, I'd rather talk about the different colors of bird poop than my life. Business and career Paige is stable. Personal life Paige … I don't even know where to start.

I spent the morning showering and getting ready with what I could. I watched TV and enjoyed every single moment of not being required anywhere. Then I went through the entire kitchen until I could find enough ingredients to possibly make Graham dinner as a thank-you.

Growing up, I used to follow Lola, our chef, around the house whenever she was there. She taught me to cook, and right now, I'm extra grateful for her patience with me as a child.

I glance at the clock. One hour. I have one hour until lunch, and he comes back. Or I assume as much anyway.

I'm not even sure if he's the kind of person who is punctual, but by how perfectly in place every single room is, I have a feeling he'll be back when he said he would. And if they really write for only a couple of hours, my time is almost up.

I pause, my hand on my hips, and take a slow turn. I am so incredibly in love with Graham's place.

Now that I think of it, though, it actually looks like he hired someone to put this place together. Whoever it was, they did an amazing job.

I know that romance books are huge right now, but there are a lot of writers out there. Graham must be a pretty darn good one.

I should have made an effort to have more conversation with him last night or even this morning. To be honest, I think the adrenaline from yesterday had worn off after my shower and the shock of what actually happened set it. For a split second, I'd forgotten about it this morning. Running like that. It's not like me to make rash choices. Or is it?

It's okay if I'm snooping for purely safety reasons. And yeah, maybe the iPad is a good thing. I can send Grace a message at least once a day, so she knows I'm safe.

I grab the iPad, type her number, and send a quick message.

Morning. It's Paige. Thank you for covering
for me yesterday. I'll call you soon.

No need to call if you can message me this
way. I'm glad you're still alive.

This guy is nice, Grace. Trust me.

Have you ever watched Dateline?

I laugh at Grace's question and then set the iPad down,
returning to my debate on whether or not I should snoop.

I move toward the big bay windows in the front room. The
natural light they bring in is beautiful, and the mountain view
is breathtaking. I've never lived in a town with mountains in
the window as if it was painted into the background.

It relaxes me.

Now, Wind Valley isn't a mountain town by any means,
but I bet it wouldn't take long to get there.

Maybe Graham will take me. He seems like a guy to enjoy
the outdoors. He did say as much this morning.

Okay, okay, enough of this *I assume* or *I think* about

Graham. It's time to cave and snoop and get to know this man. Heck, I don't even know his last name.

I spin toward the bookcase, a smile on my mouth. It's a big bookcase. I don't know why it surprises me after he admitted to being a writer. Maybe because he's a man. A big man. A man I clearly judged too quickly, because I did not expect him to be a writer and a *reader*.

Like a complete weirdo, I run my fingers over the shelf. Zane Rosey, Hero Quinn, Beck Robertson, Simon Stone, Tobias Banks, and more.

"Holy crap. He really does love romance books."

I actually laugh out loud at this.

If I were going to sneak off with a complete stranger, so far, Graham is definitely the right pick.

I step away from the white shelves that have brought me more joy than I'd expected, and then I see it. The entire bottom shelf. Books by Graham Wright.

Holy shit.

I glance back up at the shelf to the other names I saw.

Holy shit!

Another giddy squeal escapes me.

This day is just too good to be true.

Everything clicks at once. The books. Graham as an author. The other authors on his shelf. They all live here. In Wind Valley. Having a father who owns a publishing company, I've heard these names before, and this group is very popular. Their group is one of a kind.

I follow Tobias with my secret Instagram account, but he isn't big on posting pictures of his face, or anyone else's, for that matter. Which is a shame because the picture on the back of his covers is gorgeous.

He's not near as beautiful as Graham, and his eyes don't steal my breath the same way my new roommate's do, but he's attractive.

This is all just crazy. This writing group is close, and it shows.

I pick up one of Graham's books. There is a couple laughing together on the cover and a brilliant blurb on the back.

I've never read Graham's work. I wasn't lying earlier when I told him I like to read. Maybe I'll read this one first.

Okay, time to move on from the shelf and find out more about this man.

I quickly walk through his kitchen, the bathroom, his room, and into the hallway laundry room. I feel guilty, but it makes sense for someone in my position. Basically, he either has a cleaner or is a clean freak, he loves organization, he eats healthy but, per the top shelf over the fridge, has a weakness for Keebler Fudge Cookies. He's also a bed maker. It's cute. All in all, I think he's just a normal guy who keeps to himself and wants to write books.

I flop onto the couch, ready to turn the TV on while I wait for him. His iPad dings with a message. I assume it's Grace, but it's not. It's a guy named Doug.

> Still nothing from Vans. Keep your head up
> though, one of them will want your backlist.
> Just be patient.

I flip the screen over quickly. I just invaded his privacy on a whole new level.

But wait.

Did he email them after being with me yesterday or the other night or when? Is this just a coincidence?

Instead of letting the what-if ideas run wild, I look back at the text.

I let out a breath. He's been discussing this with Doug for weeks.

Another message ping comes in, but this time from Betty.

> Can't wait to see you! The girls can't wait
> for their uncle and the water park.

"For heaven's sake," I say out loud to no one and flip the tablet over again.

I put all my attention on the show on the screen.

I may as well just relax.

Relax.

A position I definitely did not see myself in today.

I settle for some documentary on Netflix and hop up for a snack.

I'm closing the cupboard when the door opens.

"I'm just leaving this painting we agreed on in his entryway, and then I'll come back later to hang it. He isn't here to tell me where it goes, and it's too big for my car. I don't want to leave it in there, and I—"

The blonde woman in the entryway sees me and freezes.

She blinks at least three times before she speaks into the phone.

"Um, I have to go," she says and then lets the phone drop. She catches it in front of her.

"Hi," she says.

I press my lips together and smile tightly.

I had no idea Graham had a girlfriend or that she'd be coming by. He never mentioned it, and I definitely feel out of place. All the chemistry I thought we had the last two days feels pretty one-sided right now.

Obviously, my need for secrecy was distraction enough for him to forget this fact too.

What is the chance she has no idea who I am?

"You're … you're Paige King."

Slim. Got it.

"Hi," I say and give a sad, flat wave.

"Oh my gosh," she says and then closes her eyes. They pop back open. "Oh yeah, you're still here."

Her playful tone makes me laugh. Of course Graham's girlfriend would be this cute.

"Yes, I am."

"In Graham's kitchen. Oh—" Her hand covers her mouth. "Oh shit, did I walk into the wrong condo?"

She looks around quickly. "Who am I kidding? Paige King wouldn't live in Wind Valley. Wait." She turns to me. "Would she?"

This time I gave her a real smile and let out a huff of a laugh.

"Temporarily, it seems. But look, I'm so sorry. I had no idea Graham had a girlfriend. He didn't do anything wrong. I put him in a position that was hard to say no to, and now I …

if I can just use your phone, I can call someone and be gone by dinner."

Just because I uprooted my life in a split moment doesn't mean I should do the same to someone else.

Her smile only widens through my mini monologue.

"I'm not Graham's girlfriend. He doesn't have one. I can't even remember the last time he dated anyone. I'm Calla Robertson. I'm married to one of his besties."

"Beck?"

She nods. "Do you know him?"

"Oh, no. I'm just putting the pieces together."

"So, Graham has told you about us?"

I shake my head.

"Not exactly. He mentioned all of you over the weekend, but nothing in detail or names."

Calla nods slowly. She steps farther into the room, extends her neck as if she's looking for someone or something.

"Do you need me to call Graham?"

"No, no, just, um—" She walks briskly down the hall and back. "I just wouldn't put it past my husband to pull a prank on me."

"With me?" I laugh.

"Oh yeah. We don't really have any limits. I once turned his hair blue." She volleys her head. "But that was when I was trying to get him to divorce me. It's a whole thing for another time."

She smiles at me and puts her hands on her hips. "I'm still a little shocked that you're standing in front of me. Are those Graham's clothes?"

I glance down at the shirt tied in a knot at my waist.

"Yeah, it's complicated, but not what you might be thinking."

Complicated, as in Graham made a more-than-gracious order of clothes off Amazon for me last night.

I let out a sigh and look up at Calla who's watching my every move. "Can I get you some water?" I ask.

It's not the first time someone has been starstruck in front of me. Which is weird. I'm not a star. I'm just some girl who was born into a wealthy family and knows no different.

"Oh shit. I'm sorry. God." She slaps her forehead. "So sorry. No, I'll leave you alone. I'm just going to leave this painting here and just, you know, um …" She spots a notepad on the counter and grabs the pen next to it. "Here is my number just in case you get tired of Graham and want someone else to hang out with. No pressure though."

She drops the pen onto the paper and moves for the door.

"You don't even know me," I say. It's clear this is my new life motto.

"No." She grins. "But if Graham trusts you to be alone in his apartment, then I know you're a good person. Outside of writers' night and me decorating this place, he keeps to himself most days and doesn't invite others over. So this is huge."

Oh, a little piece of Graham I didn't know. Maybe Calla would be good to be around after all.

"Thank you for the number. I'll use it soon. And, um, if you could not tell anyone about me, that would be great."

She makes a classic zipper gesture in front of her lips and tosses the fake key. "I won't even tell Beck. Oh god. I didn't even ask if you were okay. Are you okay? You ran out of your own wedding yesterday, and you must be … you know what? That was personal. Ignore me. Bye."

And with that, she's gone, and I'm alone again.

I turn, taking in the clean space and slowly look around. I know I snooped a little before, but a few things make sense now.

I move to the couch and turn the TV back on.

Has Graham ever had a roommate?

A girlfriend?

A longtime girlfriend?

There are no pictures and—

The iPad dings. Another text from his sister. I'm about to face it back down when I spot the notes app. Out of curiosity, I open it.

Hey, it's Graham. Are you doing okay? Can I grab you anything on the way home? Lunch? Snacks? Ice cream?

I start to type out that I don't need anything, but then I delete it and type, *nope, these fudge cookies did the trick.*

Damn. I thought I hid those well.

Not enough.

How bad did you snoop?

. . .

I would never do that.

*I would. *wink emoji**

Instead of replying, I just sit back.

He's flirting with me. I can't remember the last time anyone flirted with me. With Vincent, everything seemed rehearsed. What he said was perfect. Too perfect now that I think about it. He didn't flirt. He was blunt. I didn't think that was a bad thing, but as it turns out, I like flirting.

I like how it makes my heart race. I like how it makes me feel alive. I like how Graham makes me feel. Relaxed. Content.

He called me strong in the car yesterday, and I haven't been able to stop thinking about it.

He's right, and I can't believe I ever let myself think otherwise.

I am strong.

Which is exactly why when Graham gets home, as much as I don't want to do it, I need to call someone in my family.

My brother will probably be the best option if I don't want this bubble that I'm living in to burst.

In the meantime, I do as I said and grab a couple of cookies and settle in for a movie.

I put one of his favorite cookies in my mouth and promptly spit it out.

Ew. Yuck.

How the heck does Graham eat these?
He's lucky he's cute.

CHAPTER NINE

GRAHAM

Writing is my favorite thing in the world to do. Having friends who just so happen to have the same career and goals as me makes it that much sweeter.

We're about to call it a day on our weekly writing session when Simon groans again.

"I can't get my computer to stay hooked up to the internet." I'm the only one to acknowledge his comment. The others are still lost in thought. "Can I use your computer to check some stats on this book?" he asks.

I nod and swivel my laptop toward him. "Yeah, here. I'll go grab a couple waters."

I heard the click of keys behind me as I step into Hero's kitchen.

"Umm, G?"

"Yeah?" I peek around the fridge door at the group. "What's up?"

"We're close, right?"

I narrow my gaze and then grab two waters. The edge in his tone sounds like this is the start to a serious conversation.

"Close, as in best friends?" I ask and flop into my seat.

"Yeah, like we share stuff with each other. Even the stuff that makes us uncomfortable."

I twist the top off my water bottle and hold it to my mouth.

"Oh, man. What did you do?" I ask and take a drink.

He shakes his head.

"Not me."

He leans in close just as Tobias, Hero, and Zane all seem to pull out of whatever writing coma they were in. Writing does that to us. Especially since we all wear headphones.

"Why does your Amazon search history consist of women's thongs, clothing, charcoal face masks, and hot pink nail polish?" Simon asks.

The water in my mouth sprays over the table, sprinkling my friends, but I think they're more shocked at the question that lingers than the fact I basically just spit on them.

"What?" is the only response I come up with.

The guys shuffle quickly to stand behind me and look too.

"Lace thongs no less."

"That's a good brand of masks. Nora has it."

"Pink, really?

Simon clears his throat. "What's going on?"

I blow a raspberry with my lips and look up to the ceiling.

How the hell am I going to answer this?

"I was shopping for gifts."

"For whom?" Tobias asks loudly with a laugh and slaps my shoulder. "Are you seeing someone?"

I shake my head. "No."

"Then who are you buying thongs for?"

Ah. Yeah, well, as they all have their eyes on me, I now realize that it would have been much easier to just say yes to the previous question.

"My sister?"

Every single one of their expressions turns to disgust.

"Yeah, so let's just get back to writing." I try not to smile at how quickly I was able to shut them up. "Only about thirty minutes left before we call it a day." I might look like a creeper, but at least I can evade the situation at hand.

Telling these guys about Paige is not an option. Not today.

"Your sister had a baby three weeks ago." Simon leans back and crosses his arms. "She's not wearing thongs. I guarantee it." His left brow peeks in challenge.

Damn it, he's right.

"It's a gift for later."

"You buy your sister her underwear?"

I keep my cool. "Yep."

"I don't believe you."

"It's a whole thing, duh." I point to my computer, totally pulling every word that spills from my mouth from my ass. "It's the start of a postpartum 'love yourself' kit. Pampering if you will. Something to help her relax, and the thongs"—I nod once— "are to make her laugh in a new time of her life."

I slide my computer back in front of me and add a note in my notes app to do this, minus actually buying her thongs. It's a good idea I wish I had come up with before I had to lie about it.

"Oh, well, that's cool."

Simon seems satisfied with this answer.

"I'll get her a gift card to Loves a Brewing to add to it,"

Beck says, referring to his sister and brother-in-law's book-store café.

"I'll get something too," Simons says, and the rest of the group follows suit.

There's a little guilt eating at me for lying, but it's hard not to be happy about how lucky I got with my friends.

As soon as we're done writing, I'm back on the road to my place. Paige is there waiting for me. I've never had a woman waiting for me to come home. Is she enjoying her time alone? Is she bored?

A grin takes over, and hell, I can't remember the last time I smiled this much over a woman.

But you can't have this one.

The thought creeps in quicker than necessary.

Who's to say I can't, huh? Opposites attract all the time. Some of the best romance stories out there are because opposites attract.

Even then, it seems the only thing opposite about us is our upbringing. And where we live. And what we do for a living. And probably the cars we drive. The food we eat. The people we socialize with. The lack of cameras in my face versus the never-ending list of tabloids with her name in the headline.

Okay, so yeah. We are different.

It doesn't mean a thing.

Except, she did just get out of a relationship. Literally walked away from her wedding yesterday. How is it possible for me to keep forgetting that small yet major detail?

I pull into my parking spot and glance up at my place. It's weird driving up and seeing the light on through the living room window. Weird—but exciting.

I sling my bag over my shoulder and head up the stairs, my heart racing at the idea of being near her again.

"Do you have company?" Mrs. Mason asks, swinging her door open as soon as I reach our shared landing.

"Hi, Mrs. Mason. It's good to see you today."

"Do you have a visitor?"

"Did you see someone?" I ask.

Her gaze narrows as she clucks her tongue and returns to her apartment, closing the door in my face.

Mrs. Mason would have the entire complex aware of Paige if I had told her.

As soon as I walk through the door of my apartment, Paige shuffles into view and holds up a fudge cookie.

"Is this plastic?"

I laugh and take the cookie from her fingers as she looks at it with a wrinkled nose and makes a fake gag.

"Don't hate on the Keeblers."

"Now, I know that you were probably raised in a loving home, but that is not a cookie. It's not even close. Shoot, I can bake cookies better than that, and I cook maybe once a month."

I set my bag down, half sit on the dining table, and cross my arms. Then I nod at the kitchen, ignoring the way she unintentionally pointed out another way our lives are opposite.

"Prove it."

"That I can bake?" She stands tall, mimicking my crossed arms and holding my gaze.

Damn. I love it when she holds her own against me. I know I'm just teasing, but she won't be taking shit from anyone, and I'm here for it.

I rise, take a step forward, and tower over her.

"Yeah, bake me something."

Her gaze remains locked on mine, even as she narrows her eyes.

"I should have something smart to say to you, but honestly, I feel like you're doubting my skills, and now I have to bake something to prove you wrong."

I hold up my hands in surrender. "I said no such thing."

She backs up and grabs a spatula from the wooden holder on the counter, pointing it at me. "You implied it with your smug face."

I bark out a laugh.

"My smug face?"

"Yep."

She starts to open and close drawers, pulling out everything she needs as if she's lived here for longer than a day. When I made the joke earlier about her snooping, I didn't mean it. But shit, I think she very well may have.

My lips twitch. If I were a woman who looked like Paige, and I decided to move in with a stranger on a whim, I'd be going through his stuff too. It makes me a little proud to know that she's smart enough to get to know her environment.

It's the safest one she can find, but in her shoes, learning that on your own means something.

"I can feel you staring at me."

I look away quickly, my gaze landing on the iPad at the table. This time, I let myself give a full-blown smile. The Bluetooth keyboard for my iPad is sitting with the propped-up device. I know for a fact that was in my room when I left earlier.

"How did the iPad work out today?"

"Oh, great. That was a nice idea. Thank you. Is it okay if I keep using it for a while? I messaged Grace today, and it was nice to have a friend."

She starts measuring the flour as I set up my computer. "That works for me. When I leave in a couple of days, it'll give us a way to communicate. I'm going to order some sandwiches online and then walk down the street to get them. What do you want?"

"Just what you get is fine."

I place the order quickly, and just as I'm standing to see if she needs help, I spot a painting I know wasn't there when I left.

"Where did that come from?"

"Oh, right, Calla stopped by."

"Calla stopped by. Did you talk to her?"

"How else would I know her name is Calla?"

"Are you okay? Did she say anything to upset you? Did she grill you about yesterday?"

Calla is the sweetest of the bunch, but Paige wanted to remain unseen. Having one of my friends randomly show up because I forgot to tell her not to drop by was a mistake on my part.

"Whoa, calm down. She was more than polite, and she honestly only offered her number in case I wanted a friend who isn't you. She was really sweet."

Like earlier, a sense of pride for my close group of friends hits me.

"I did swear her to secrecy, though. I'm still not sure what I'm doing next. I mean, I know I will go home eventually, but until then, it's best to lay low. That said, can I borrow your phone to call my brother?"

"You have a brother?"

She nods and stirs the dough. "I do. His name is Preston. He's basically the male version of me. You'd like him."

"Cool" is all I say, because sure I might like him … up until he convinces her to leave. Honestly, this is all starting to feel too good to be true. Who just meets a runaway bride, invites her to live at his place, and gets lucky enough that the entire thing is fate?

Holy shit. What am I saying?

I write way too many romance novels.

"Yeah, here's my phone." I set it on the counter by the toaster oven. "I'm going to go get lunch. Be right back."

"Okay, thanks again."

"Anytime," I say and walk out the door, giving her privacy to talk to her brother and giving myself some air.

Something about her makes me feel like a different man. A foolish man, clearly.

I mean, come on, the world's most loved socialite daughter falls for a small-town romance writer is the plotline to a novel, not real life.

Not mine, anyway.

In fact, once I'm gone, and she's here alone, I doubt she'll last long. She'll go home, and I'll come back to an empty apartment.

And then I move forward right back to the rut I've been in.

Life is going *great*.

CHAPTER TEN
PAIGE

I waited till morning to call my brother, and even though the little temperature thing on Graham's patio says it's only seventy-one degrees out, I'm sweating like it's one hundred. Don't even get me started on how badly my heart is hammering in my chest. This is just one of two big things I'm doing today.

I feel like what I assume being sent to the principal's office would feel like if I had ever been sent there. Attending a private school where your father donated more than any other family, well, you could get away with murder.

Not that I was a bad student, because I wasn't, but you get the—

"Hello?" my brother's hesitant voice fills the line.

I sit up straight on the sofa, as if he can see me.

"Hi, it's me."

"Holy shit," he says and then the line goes muffled as he says, "Excuse me, I have to take this."

A moment later, I hear a door click, and then he's

bombarding me with questions. "Holy fuck, Paige. Where are you? Are you okay? What happened? It's been three days. Why didn't you call me sooner? I'm your brother, you should have told me the morning of, and I would have snuck you out. Wait, whose number is this?"

I don't answer a single question.

"Did I interrupt a meeting?" I ask. Preston is older than me by three years and is proudly following in our father's footsteps to take over everything so my dad can retire. He deserves it, too. My dad tried to offer him his role right out of high school, but Preston wanted to earn it. He's done more years in college than most of my father's board members, and he still takes courses to stay up to date on trends.

"No way. We are not talking about me right now. I only answered because no one has heard from you and the area code was a Wyoming number, which so happens to be the last place I saw my sister, so my hopes were high. Now, spill. Do I need to send a plane for you?"

I sigh heavily.

"No."

"Where's your phone?"

"The last place I saw it was in the bridal suite."

"Figures. I'm so mad at you right now, but fuck, Paige, I feel like I haven't caught my breath in days. You're my best friend. How could you not tell me where you were? Or not tell anyone?"

"I talked to Grace."

"Of course you did, and of course she lied to my face when I asked her about it."

"Were you nice when you asked?"

"I'm always nice."

"Not to Grace."

"Especially Grace."

"Since when? You two have been at each other's throats since we were kids."

"That's not the point right now."

"Right."

"Are you okay?" his voice goes soft again. "Like really?"

"Honestly, yes."

"Do you want to tell me what happened?"

I let out a sigh. I almost follow it up with another one because I'm so tired of sighing. I feel like that's all I do unless Graham is here.

"Vincent told me the night before that cheated on me."

"That fucking bastard. I'm going to beat his ass."

I laugh. "Yeah, okay."

"What? I could."

'I'm not saying you couldn't, but that's not you."

"Maybe not, but he hurt you, and that's not okay."

"I don't see it that way."

"Come on, Paige, really."

"I see it more like he saved me from making a giant mistake. Obviously, I haven't spoken to him, but I think … I think he knew if either of us were going to do the right thing, it would be me."

"Oh, and running without talking to anyone was the right thing?"

"No, but not marrying him was."

The famous King sigh fills the line.

"Where are you?"

"I'm, um, staying with a friend."

"Who?"

"I'm safe, Pres, okay. Trust me."

I can practically hear him rolling his eyes over the phone.

"Tell me or I'll just have someone trace this number, and I'll show up unannounced and drag you back here where I can physically see that you're safe."

He did this one in high school, so I believe his threat. It's the reason my dad assigned me my own security.

"His name is Graham Wright. And like I said, I'm safe here. Hey, is Turner okay? He didn't get fired, did he?"

"That's what you're worried about?"

"Yes."

"He's fine. He's on leave until further notice, but he still has a job. Whatever Grace told Dad after she viewed the security tapes is the only reason you aren't back home right now."

"Good. Make sure he keeps his job after you tell Mom and Dad you talked to me."

"What? No. I'm not calling them."

"Please. If I talk to them, they'll convince me to come home, and I don't want to do that yet. I need time to figure myself out."

"When do you plan on coming home?"

"I don't know."

"Paige …"

"I know. I just … I don't know, either. Only a few people know I'm here. It's nice to just be me. I don't want to leave yet."

"All right, I get it. For now anyway. Do you have money or anything? Can I send you a new phone and your cards at least? That way, if something goes south with this so-called friend, you have options and a way to reach me."

I laugh a little.

"It sort of feels like I'm talking to my dad right now, but sure. Graham has paid for some clothes and stuff to get me by these last few days, but I can't expect him to pay for me much longer."

"Does he know who you are?"

"Yes."

"And he's cool paying for stuff?"

"Not everyone wants to be in our life for money, Pres."

"Maybe not, but those people are pretty fucking rare to find."

"Which is exactly why I want to stay here for a little while longer."

"Fuck, Paige, I'm glad you called me. I came to work to distract my brain, but I was worried. Worried and proud—is that a thing?"

"It is now."

"Seriously though, call Dad soon. I'll reach out to him this afternoon."

"I will. Just as soon as you send me my phone."

"Amber!" he shouts to his assistant. "Come in here."

"Don't make her do it right now."

"I am, but then I need to get back to this meeting. I'm glad you're safe and, Paige, don't wait too long to come home. Avoiding everyone isn't going to make it go away."

"I know."

"Good. Okay, I love you."

"Wait, I didn't even give you an address."

"Don't need one. I looked up Graham Wright's while we were talking and got his address right here. Google is a scary thing. Now, enjoy small-town life, but come back to your real one soon."

"Okay. Thank you."

"And Paige."

"Yeah?"

"I'm so fucking happy you didn't marry Vincent."

I feel guilty when I smile. "Me too."

He clicks off the line before I can actually say the words.

Guilt is a weird thing. It can go so many different ways.

Being alone for most of yesterday morning did give me time to think about Vincent and the wedding, and I hate to admit this, but my heart had checked out a long time ago. I clearly just needed his admission for my brain to figure out what my next move was. So yeah, I feel guilty that I'm not upset over not getting married. I feel guilty that my mind has already been filled with thoughts of another man. I feel guilty that I made promises to people when, until a few days ago, I never knew how much I didn't mean them.

I blow out a breath. You know what? I'm done feeling guilty. I'm done doing what I think everyone else thinks is the right thing. I just want to do what I want, and from here on out, that's exactly what I'm going to do.

I walk back to the bookshelf in the living room. I know it's silly, but I love seeing it. Especially since I started reading one of Graham's books. It gave me an idea.

I move farther into the condo and find Graham predictably sitting at the kitchen table with his computer in front of him. He's lit a cinnamon candle—that's my favorite smell. He's got on a pair of headphones and looks hard at work. He's so focused that he doesn't even see me standing in my doorway. He doesn't see me staring at his bare chest.

This has to be said again. I cannot for the life of me get over how sexy this man is. He's got a candle lit, two drinks in front of him, a coffee and a water. A bowl of the coconut snack things he loves next to the drinks. He's shirtless, and his hair is sticking up as if he's been pulling on it. He smirks and leans back, pulling one arm up to rest on the back of his chair. It draws my gaze to his muscles, to the veins screaming at me to run my fingers over them until I have them memorized.

"How long are you going to stand there?" he asks, sliding the headphones down to his shoulders.

Are romance writers supposed to be this attractive? He's the perfect blend of confidence and cocky. And he knows it.

"Paige," he says my name again, but this time it sounds like a warning.

I snap out of it and take a seat next to him.

"You leave in less than a week, right?"

He nods. "Are you going to be okay here alone?"

"Yep, except I was thinking I'd go with you."

"What?" He huffs a laugh. "No."

"Why not?"

"Because"—he spins his computer to face me—"everyone is still guessing where you are. If you and I step out there together and someone sees you, boo! Our personal lives are all over the media. That might be part of your life, but it's not mine."

"Come on, Graham." I hold up his book. "I'm making a bucket list like your heroine in this book did. I want to spend the next however many weeks you're on the road experiencing things I've never done."

"You don't need me for that."

"Sure I do. I don't know anyone else, and if I ask someone I do know, they'll do it the way I've done everything. I want to do it your way."

"My way?"

"Yes. You live so carefree, but you're still successful and passionate about what you do. I want that. I *need* that balance. Shoot, being here for only a couple days has been so relaxing. I need you to show me how to do that forever."

He blows out his breath.

"I'm not going on some joy ride though. I'm going to book signings and to see my sisters and their kids. It's not going to be fancy. You'll have theme parks and pools and all the things kids ten and under want to do."

"I'm sure we can make time for things on my list. It's not like I'm asking you to climb Mount Everest."

He shakes his head. "I'll be back and forth on the road between here and all these other places for like four weeks. I don't want the media following me that long."

"If you take me with you, I'll talk to my dad."

His gaze snaps to mine, and his jaw ticks.

"What?"

"I didn't do it on purpose, okay, but I saw your texts with Doug. You want a contract with my dad's company. I can help with that."

I don't include the part where I have no say in what the company does or that my dad is probably furious with me right now, but those are all things I can fix later. After Graham agrees and takes me with him.

"That's it? I just take you with me?"

"Yes, and, you know, do things with me. Like friends on a road trip checking off a list."

"This seems too easy."

"You've never spent four weeks with me before."

"Is this you trying to convince me to say yes?"

"Please." I press my palms together and smile at him.

"It's a nice offer, but I keep thinking of the media, and I just don't want that."

"Okay, I get it. But getting your books on international shelves or into theaters or whatever other doors Vans can give you is what you want. You can keep busting your ass trying or spend four weeks with me and possibly reach this goal by the end of the year."

He groans.

"Just so we're clear, all I have to do is let you come with me and go along with all your bucket list items, and you'll convince your dad to contract my books?"

"Yep."

"Deal."

I stick out my hand to shake on it and then bounce back to my room to get the notebook I stole from his kitchen yesterday. It has my list.

I cross off the only thing on it: convince Graham to take me on a road trip.

Now, time to make the rest of it.

If I'm going to find out what kind of life I want, I've only got four weeks.

I better make it count.

CHAPTER ELEVEN

GRAHAM

It's crazy how fast life can change. This time last week, I was loading my car with my weekend clothes, ready to watch Zane propose to Willa. I'd planned to do my part as his best friend, get some writing in, and then come home. That was it.

Of course, then I had to go ahead and tell myself that it was time to take risks. To do things that put me out of my comfort zone. Now I'm getting my morning word count in before Paige and I load up my car and hit the road. Our first stop is Denver for a signing and to see my oldest sister.

A road trip with the Forbes Princess is definitely outside of my box. Guess I at least accomplished that part.

The shower in the spare bath turns off as I pour myself some coffee.

I move back to the table, set my cup down, and adjust the computer.

Since Paige moved in and some of the clothes we ordered for her showed up, we've created a pretty steady routine in the morning. Well, for the entire day, if you really think about it. She runs with me in the morning, and then when I go to the complex gym, she heads back here and cooks breakfast. Typically, she's already in her room getting ready for the day when I get back, but she always leaves me a plate.

It's the most mundane morning routine in the world, but fuck all if something about it doesn't make me feel good.

To say that leaving today couldn't have come at a better time is an understatement. I'm hoping that by being forced to be in a car with her and spend every moment with her, whatever attraction I have for her and this enjoyment of her living with me will vanish.

I scrub my hand over my face and debate typing out a text to Doug.

What could I even say that wouldn't give away her location? Which, to be clear, Paige and I going on a road trip puts her back out there. Someone will see us. As soon as we get in the car, I need to find out her clear goals. Yeah, maybe she'll hate that I ask so many questions and want to call this off.

But fuck. If she does, then bye-bye Vans.

I have no idea how to play this.

As soon as she asked to come with me the other day, no was my only answer—but her offer! Hell, how was I supposed to turn that down? Okay, sure, going on a road trip with a woman who I'm not dating isn't exactly fulfilling my personal goals, but this trip could advance my career by months. There is no way I couldn't take it. I have to. She knew exactly how to get me to cave.

It's safe to say that I might not know what I'm getting myself into. But, for the sake of my career, I better get on board with whatever she wants.

"I don't have much," she says, popping out of her room. "But I'm ready."

She pulls my spare suitcase behind, and I glance at the clock.

"All right. Let's go."

I pack my laptop quickly and load everything into the car. Once she's in and has her seat belt on, I hand her a notebook and a pen.

"What's this?"

"A place to write out all your bucket list items."

She smiles. "You bought me this? You're really trying to butter me up before I call my dad, aren't you?"

I laugh. "Actually, I just thought you'd rather have a full notebook instead of my grocery list notepad. It was an extra. I didn't make any special trips for you."

"Someone is observant" is all she says.

She flips it open and writes Paige's Bucket List at the top.

Then she taps the pen against the blank page.

I climb into the driver's seat and turn on music but notice how she doesn't write anything down. It isn't until we're on the interstate that I speak up.

"What do you have so far?"

She grabs her purse and pulls out the page ripped from my kitchen notepad and shows me.

One single line is crossed out.

"That's it?"

"Well, I wasn't sure you'd say yes, so I didn't want to get my hopes up."

"You didn't add anything over the last few days?"

She shakes her head.

"Okay, let's make a list while I drive."

My stress level might go down a notch if I know some of the things she wants me to do with her. I have no idea what it means to find yourself with someone like her. Hell, I've known who I was since before I can remember. She could have crazy ideas, and I need to be prepared for them.

"Okay. How about doing something crazy?"

"Too vague," I say and point at myself. "Plus, taking a road trip with a stranger would cross that off already."

"I kind of want to write it just to cross it off." She laughs.

"Look at that. You're getting to know yourself already. You're a list girl."

"Don't make fun of me."

"I'm not. You're looking at the king of lists. I even made one to pack my bag this morning."

"No, you didn't."

"Sure did."

She smiles, but then looks back at the road. "Well, what do I put then?"

"This is your list, not mine."

"I need help. What's the craziest thing you've ever done?"

I laugh instantly.

"Oh, it's that good, huh?"

"Tobias and I once released a book on the same day and made a bet on who could sell more. The loser had to streak through campus during orientation. It definitely took my mind off the lack of book sales."

She lets out the cutest laugh I've ever heard.

"I'm not doing that."

"Obviously. You're not in college."

"Getting naked in front of a lot of people, I mean. But! What if I get naked and no one sees me?"

"I'm pretty sure you do that every day before you shower. All right. What's next?" I ask, changing the subject from any conversation of her naked. "What is one thing you've always wanted to do but never had the chance because of your family's reputation or your bodyguards?"

"Sing karaoke or set off a firework or color my hair purple. Oh! Or go camping in like an actual tent—ooh, ooh, or adopt a pet or plant my own garden or—"

"Don't tell me. Use that pen. If it's not on the list, it won't happen."

If these are the things she wants to do, the next three weeks are going to be a piece of cake.

"Oh shoot," she says after all the things are added to the list. "We were supposed to get snacks."

"For what?"

"This road trip. I searched online for the best ways to make a road trip fun, and every article said to buy snacks."

I can't help it; I let out a laugh. "We can stop and get them at the next town, because you're right: this trip is downright awful without them."

"Stop." She shoves my shoulder. "It's my first road trip."

"You're kidding."

"Nope. My dad always said travel time is like losing time off your life, so we fly everywhere."

I get what he means, but never a road trip? Ever?

No wonder she was so eager to go with me. She might have experienced a lot in her life, but I have a feeling the list of things she hasn't done is just as long.

I'm doing this so she'll get me in with her dad's company, but a part of me takes joy in knowing that I get to be the one to show her all these things.

I'll be the guy she thinks of when she looks back on this moment years from now.

She'll probably laugh, thinking how crazy she was to think a few weeks with a stranger was going to change everything.

I'm okay with that, because years from now, when I'm on the set for one of my books or in Paris at a book signing, I'll think back and know that this crazy woman helped me change my life.

CHAPTER TWELVE
PAIGE

My ass hurts.

I had no idea that it would be a thing for a road trip, yet here I am, ready for him to pull off the road at our hotel. I'm hoping it's one with a spa. He mentioned having a book signing this afternoon, so in order to stay discreet, hiding out with a massage sounds like a genius idea.

"What time is your signing?" I ask. We've spent so much time talking about me and the things I want to do that I want to make sure he gets to do the things he wants to do, too.

"At 2:00. Once we get to the hotel, I need to check in and then go to the room where the signing is. Doug just moved to Denver last year, so I've had all my stuff shipped to him, and he set up my table earlier today."

"Ooh, that's royal treatment."

"Tell me about it. It's not a common thing, but I lucked out with him as an agent."

"I'll say."

He taps the wheel and then clears his throat.

"How do you plan to get into the room without being seen?"

"By following you and keeping my head down."

"Do you think that will work?"

"Maybe you'll let me borrow your sunglasses?"

He smiles, and I swear it makes my heart beat faster.

We've been in this car for almost four hours and one thing is clearer than ever before. Being with Graham is different. It makes me feel different. I don't worry or think the worst of a situation that hasn't happened yet. I don't feel the need to say the right thing at every moment. I can ask questions, and he doesn't make me feel dumb with his answers.

"How long are we here?"

"For the entire weekend, but only one night at the hotel and one with my sister. She lives about an hour outside of Denver."

"Why don't you just stay with her the whole time?"

"I like to stay at the same hotel as the convention. Makes it easier, and I get to interact with readers. Which reminds me. Unless you decide you want to be seen today, you'll probably just be in the room."

"No problem. I was going to see if they have a spa or something."

"They don't. I checked this morning."

I cross my arms and twist to face him. "You checked this morning?"

"Yep."

"Why? Are you a spa guy?"

"Nope, but I don't want you to get bored."

How cute is that? But then I remember my end of the deal. Of course he'll do all the things to keep me happy.

I grab his iPad and log into my email account. I type out my dad's email address, but that's it. If I'm even going to attempt this for Graham, I should probably call my dad first. Hearing from me after almost a week through email might not be the best way to go about it.

So I just log out and shut off the iPad. It turns out to be good timing because Graham pulls into the hotel valet.

He hands me his sunglasses and gives me a look. I nod, and we both get out.

Less than a week and I can already read his mind. Damn.

The valet gets our bags, gives us a ticket, and we go inside. Not a single person has pointed me out or put a camera in my face.

The door guys open the door and smile. "Welcome, miss."

"Thank you."

I step inside and look back. The valet has moved on to the next guest.

"Huh, I was thinking it might be more eventful than that."

"Me too, but I'm glad it's not."

If that's how easy it is here, maybe I can do something other than hang out in the room.

Graham hands over his information at the reception desk to check in.

"One or two keys?" the man asks.

"Oh shit. I didn't even think to call for a second room." Graham sounds panicked. "I ... can we get two rooms?"

"Sorry, Mr. Wright, the entire hotel is booked for the convention."

"It's fine," I say quickly. "We've lived together the past week. This will be no different."

"It'll be completely different," Graham deadpans.

I hold back my smile as I turn to the guy behind the counter. "One room is fine. Can we get one with two beds?"

"The reservation only has one king."

"Perfect," I say as to not draw attention.

Once we have our keys, we head up to our room.

The door closes behind us, and I just know Graham is about to apologize so I beat him to it.

"Damn. I wish I had 'share a bed with a guy I met a week ago' on my list."

My comment earns me the laugh I'd been aiming for.

"I think the couch pulls out," he says.

"Stop. I think we can be adults. It's one night."

"Right. Okay, well, I'm going to freshen up and head downstairs. The signing is from two to six, so I could bring dinner back after if you want. Or you can order room service, or you can—"

"I'll be fine."

"I know."

His gaze stays on me a moment longer, and then he does exactly as he said and leaves me in the room. I should have told him how hot he looked in just a simple shirt and jeans, but he already seemed on edge about sharing a bed. I don't want to make it worse. But seriously, jeans on that man … whoa.

I wait until precisely two o'clock and slip out of the room myself. Most people will be at the signing, so I should be able to sneak around the hotel unnoticed easily.

I head down the elevator, and as soon as the doors open and I step out, I stop.

Normally at this point, I'd have someone pointing to

where I'm supposed to go or making sure my route is clear. Right now, though, it's my choice.

Not leaving the hotel is probably the smartest since I don't have a phone to reach Graham if anything happens. I mean, I have plenty of other numbers memorized, but that's a worst-case scenario.

A group of women pass me, pulling little tote things behind them. There are a few books in each—are they going to the signing? It's not my plan to go there, but honestly, these readers are here to find new books. No one is going to expect Paige King to show up.

Just in case, though, I stop in at the little store in the lobby and buy a hat, charging it to the room.

Hope Graham's cool with that.

Next, I head for the conference room.

"Hi, can I help you?" A woman stops me.

"I'm just going in there," I say and point to a room full of tables and people rushing around.

"Do you have a ticket?"

"A ticket?"

"Yes. To go to the signing."

"Can you charge it to my room?"

The woman smiles but shakes her head. "I'm afraid not."

"Okay, that's fine, I ..." My words trail off when I spot Graham in a corner. He's got a line of people in front of him and is taking a picture with a couple of readers.

I press my lips together, but it doesn't stop the smile. Again, why does he have to be so damn cute? He's all man, but he just does these cute things, and it makes me feel things I shouldn't.

We are in two completely different spots in our lives. It

doesn't make sense for me to look at him this way after knowing him for such a short time.

"I'm sorry, miss, but can you step aside to let these folks in?"

I do as she asks.

"Sorry about that."

The readers all show a badge thing and then go into the room.

"Was there a specific author you wanted to see?"

I shake my head. "No."

"Oh," she says, and I can hear it in her voice that she's confused why I'm here if I'm not here to see an author.

"My friend is signing, but I'll just see him after. Thank you."

I head back down the hall toward the bar and lobby.

I wish I had a phone right now. I'd call my dad and get that awkward conversation over with just so I could ask him to look into Graham. I only watched him for a moment, but after reading one of his books and seeing him with his readers just now, Vans would be perfect for him.

I take a breath and head back to the room.

I should add attending a book signing to my list.

Graham would get a kick out of it. Then he'd tease me because, for as much as I don't want to be seen, the things I want to do make that impossible.

It's funny. The moment I ran out in my wedding dress, I wanted nothing more than to be invisible, but now, if Graham is with me, I don't mind being seen.

CHAPTER THIRTEEN
GRAHAM

I slept on the couch.

It didn't pull out either, and my height did pose an issue for most of the night, but I'd do it again.

Last night was déjà vu. I brought dinner back to the room, and Paige and I sat in front of the TV watching movies like we did the very first night we met. Normally, I like to spend the night after a signing attending the events and connecting with readers, but I won't take back last night for anything.

Nothing even remotely exciting happened either.

Once she fell asleep on the couch, her head on my shoulder, I may have watched her long enough to see the two freckles she has right under her left ear. She also has a small dot of a scar right under her chin, but I only noticed that one after I carried her to the bed and tucked her in.

Did I debate crawling in on the other side? Yes.

She told me at least three times between yawning last night that it wasn't going to bother her. It was a big enough bed. But I couldn't bring myself to do it.

Yesterday morning, I started my day with the plan of … hell, I didn't really have a plan. Make her happy so she'll talk to her dad. Make her happy because I like her smile. Because I can't imagine living a life that holds you back from experiencing anything. But then I went to the signing, and I missed her. I wished she'd been there.

Fuck. What does that mean?

I sit up slowly and run a hand over my face. I glance at the bed where she's still sleeping. I don't want to wake her, so I grab my laptop off the floor next to me.

I should get some words in, but honestly, I stayed up late doing just that, and something keeps creeping back in my mind.

I pull up Google and type in Paige King sightings.

I scroll for about ten minutes and rephrase the question at least three times.

Nothing pulls up for Denver.

I let out my breath and lean back.

It's not the end of the world if I somehow managed to get into a picture with her. I just don't want my face blasted everywhere. I have no big story or history that led me to this choice, just have my own opinion. I want my name to be known, not my face. Not what I do in my personal life or who I'm seen with. Just the books and the fact that I keep producing them.

Would being seen with Paige King bring me an audience I might not have had before? Sure. But that's not how I want to gain new readers.

I've worked so hard for so long on building things myself that the idea of my career progressing because of who I'm associated with instead of the books themselves feels wrong.

"Of course you're awake and writing already. You write, work out, eat, repeat."

It's eight in the morning, and she's teasing me already.

"I like writing and working out and eating, so I do them."

She rolls her eyes with a smile.

"What's the plan today?"

I stand, running a hand over my head, and step for the bathroom.

"Well, up until your comment, it was hit the road to my sister's, but now you should tell me. If you could have a routine of your own in the morning, what would it be?"

Her eyes widen, and she takes in my appearance. Her eyes move slowly from my face down to where I'm wearing only a pair of navy boxer briefs.

Shit. Forgot about that.

"I ..." She starts and then smiles. "Do you really want to know?"

With that hungry look in her eyes? No, not really. A man can only have so much self-control when there's a beautiful woman in the bed next to him who just turned her flirting up a notch. I can't have her but having her here has a purpose.

"I do."

She smirks, studies me for a moment. Her gaze holds me in place as all the ideas of what she could be thinking run through my mind.

"I want"—she pauses, never breaking eye contact with me — "a big ... hot ... chocolate chip pancake."

She falls back against the pillows with a laugh, and I shake my head.

"Ha, ha, laugh it off." I march into the bathroom. "You still have to ride in a car with me."

I close the door, listening to her sweet laugh from the other side.

A smile touches my lips as I start the shower. I know I shouldn't think it, but waking up to her face and her voice and that sound is really fucking nice.

It just seals my decision that I'm ready to settle down. As soon as these next four weeks are up, it's game on.

I shower quickly and then order room service while Paige is getting ready. She successfully stuffs her face, and we have everything loaded into the car by midmorning. We'll be at my sister's house a lot sooner than planned, but right now, having other people around us is probably the best choice. Too much alone time with Paige and loving how well we get along plays tricks on my mind. I need a distraction.

I start the car but don't move yet.

"Okay, before we head out of the city, let me see that list." I reach for it, but she jerks it back.

"No."

"Why not? We made it yesterday. I just need a refresher."

"Then I'll read it to you."

Her cheeks start to flush, and I lean back.

"Paige King, did you add something to the list last night that you don't want me to see?"

She nods once. "A few things."

"What are they?"

"Mmm, no. They're for me only."

"How can I help you if you don't tell me?"

She lets out a sigh and locks her gaze on mine.

"Do not comment on them," she says and hands me the list.

I browse through it quickly, taking note of the ones I

remember from yesterday. Yep, there are three new lines at the bottom:

Attend a book signing.

Ride a roller coaster.

Skinny-dip.

I snap my gaze to hers, but I don't say a word.

That is, until I decide that we can cross one of these off before we go to my sister's house.

"Six Flags it is."

"What?"

"If you want a theme park with a roller coaster, there's one here, and we can cross that one off today."

"Oh, already? Isn't that a bit extreme for one of the first ones? How about fishing?"

I shake my head. "We can go camping and fish later. Today we're going to ride some rides."

I pull onto the road and enter the address for Six Flags into my navigation.

"I'm not so sure about this." She sets the list in her lap and scratches at her neck as she looks it over.

"Okay, we can skip it and just go to my sister's place. No big deal. You only have three weeks. We can totally do something else, and when you go home at the end of the month and—"

"Okay, okay, let's go."

I smile with victory and keep that smile until we're standing in line at the biggest roller coaster in the park. The coaster train races by us, and I swear I see Paige's hair move.

Fuck. Maybe I oversold this. I can't remember the last time I was on one of these things. Maybe the county fair where I went on the Tilt-a-Whirl and proceeded to vomit on one of my sisters, who then refused to take me with her each year after that.

"Are you ready?" Paige asks.

"Totally."

I'll never let her know my real thoughts.

"Me too. Let's do this."

The ride attendant checks our wristbands and points to which seats to take. Another attendant assists until we are securely locked in place. Other riders are laughing and clapping. A kid behind us says he can't wait to see his picture at the end and hopes it's a good one. He even tells his friend they should hold peace signs the entire time to get it on film.

Okay, you hold a peace sign. My eyes will be securely shut while I picture myself being anywhere but here.

"Everyone all set?" the man behind the control yells. It seems everyone yells yes but me and Paige. I look over at her and her brows raise like she's excited, and she smiles.

The ride starts to move, and her hand grabs mine. She grips it so hard; I feel one of my fingers pop.

"Paige," I start, but she shakes her head and closes her eyes.

We keep inching forward.

I watch us climb the first hill and then notice the drop over it.

"This is a bad idea," I say, the panic evident in my voice.

"I don't think I'm a roller coaster person," Paige follows up with just as much fear in her tone.

"I puked on the last ride I was on."

"And you're just now telling me."

I press my eyes closed.

"It didn't seem important till now."

"You owe me when this is over."

"I know." I squeeze her hand as we drop.

I don't know who screams more between the two of us, but as soon as the ride comes to a stop, we look at each other and burst into laughter.

We make it down the steps and agree to get back on the road just before I proceed to throw up in the nearest trash can.

You win some, you lose some, but seeing her smile as we walk out the gate makes it all worth it.

CHAPTER FOURTEEN
PAIGE

"I think it's safe to say that we can take thrill seekers off the list of things I like," I say and sip on the cherry Pepsi Graham got me from the gas station.

"I agree." He nods. "I can take it off my list too."

"Oh, Mr. Wedding Crasher has a limit on the thrills?"

He chuckles and then glances over at me. I can't tell if it's the way his arms hang over the wheel, his backward hat, or the fact we just shared a memory I'll never ever forget, but I really really want to kiss him right now.

"That was a one-and-done kind of situation. I was looking for a little excitement in life that night."

"Well, you found it," I say and happily cross the roller coaster off my list. "I bet you didn't think you'd end up on a road trip with me after that night."

"Nope."

"I know why I'm looking for excitement right now, but why were you?"

We might not be that different after all.

He rubs his neck.

"To be honest, I love a routine, but so far in my life, routine hasn't really brought me the best of luck when it comes to love. So yeah, I was forcing myself to step out of my box."

"And you got a runaway bride. Lucky you."

I mean it as a joke, but he doesn't laugh, so I change the subject quickly.

"I put roller coaster on my list because a kid from one of my foundations used to talk about them all the time. He loved them, so I wanted to see what the fuss was about. It fit his personally perfectly."

I can feel Graham's stare even though he doesn't say anything,

"What?" I ask and my cheeks start to warm.

He shakes his head. "Nothing."

"Say it."

"I just think that's awesome. You put that on your list because you were thinking of someone else. From what I saw, I have a good feeling that a lot of things on your list came from the same place."

I shrug. "Maybe. Most are my own, though."

"Oh, I know. Skinny-dipping," he says with a laugh.

"I said don't comment," I say and slug his shoulder. Still, I can't hide the smile that touches my lips as I look out the window.

He steers the car around another corner, and we pull up to a gated community. He slows as a guard comes to his window.

"Mr. Wright. It's good to see you again. Your sister told

me you were coming today. Can I help you with anything before you go in?"

"No, sir. Thank you."

The guard steps back and waves us through.

"What is this place?"

"This is where my sister lives."

"It looks nice."

"It is. Her husband is one of the best surgeons in the Rocky Mountains."

"Wow. And what does she do?"

"She used to be a lawyer, but now she stays home with the kids. They have four of them. The youngest is only a couple of weeks old."

"Oh, and she's fine with visitors?"

I've never held a newborn, and the idea that maybe I will this weekend makes my heart race. I quickly add it to the list.

I don't have a lot of friends with kids and when I visit those who do, the babies are with the nanny. It always seemed weird to me because watching babies see or do something for the first time has always made my heart happy. There isn't anything wrong with having a nanny, but I think I'd be a no-nanny person.

I take another look at the list. Maybe I should add things to do after the three weeks. If I really am a list person, maybe having them on paper will hold me to it.

"This is it," Graham says, pulling into a long driveway. A large white brick house with blue trim comes into view. It looks rustic and cozy from the outside. There's clearly a guesthouse in the back and a pool.

There are trees all around the house, and once we pull up to the front doors, it's clear you can't even see the main road anymore. Everything is just so green. I love everything about it.

"Ready?" Graham asks, and I nod. He gets out and comes around to my door.

"I'm nervous," I admit as he pulls me to his side before his hand settles on my lower back. I take a breath and look at him. He turns at the same time, and we're so close our noses almost touch.

He clears his throat and steps back.

"They're going to love you. My sister has been a fan of yours since she was little, so go easy on her if she fangirls too hard."

"I doubt that but thank you for making me feel better."

"I'm serious. I'm pretty sure she tried to recreate an outfit of yours for prom once." He chuckles. "I'm pretty sure it was the poor man's version, but she was happy with it."

I shove him. "I bet it was beautiful. Next time she has somewhere to go, I'll be happy to loan her one of my dresses. I have a closet at home full of too many dresses to count that will never be worn again."

There's a small stiffness to his posture, but he relaxes just as the door to his sister's house opens.

"Oh shit. You're here."

"Betty, seriously?"

"I don't know how I'm supposed to act, Graham."

"Like an adult. Say hi or something."

"Hi." His sister beams a smile at me. The quick banter between them reminds me of Preston. I miss him.

"Hi. It's so good to meet you and thank you so much for letting me join Graham for the weekend."

"It's nothing compared to what you're used to, so I hope

you don't mind a good old-fashioned night of homemade pizza and wings off the smoker."

Her gaze flicks to Graham's for a moment. I get the sense that she's worried about the night.

"Do you have blue cheese dressing?" I ask.

Graham makes a gagging noise, and his sister grins. "Sure do."

"Then tonight will be perfect."

"Mom, who is it? Don't just stand at the door waiting for them to pull into the driveway. That's weird."

A smaller version of his sister steps into view, and her eyes go wide.

"I take that back. It's more weird that you won't let her in."

"Oh, right, yes."

His sister moves for us to step inside.

"I hate that she's smarter than me sometimes."

"Sometimes? Try all the time, Mom."

"And that would be my cue to introduce you to my mini me. This is Lexi. She's seventeen and thinks she knows everything."

"Seventeen, wow. I didn't realize the two of you were so far apart in age," I say.

"We aren't," Graham replies. "My sister was a teen mom. She had Lexi at fifteen."

"Oh, wow."

"And then we got married and had three more beautiful babies, including this one."

A tall man walks in with the smallest little human I've ever seen cradled in his arms. "Hi, I'm Ben."

"It's nice to meet you."

"It only took him four tries to get a boy." Graham laughs and walks past into the kitchen. As soon as I step into the space, it's clear that there isn't an ounce of counter space that isn't used.

"They go all-out," Graham says quickly. "I can see by the look on your face that you're questioning what's happening."

"Do they always do this?"

He nods. "She gets it from our parents."

"Even for just two extra people?"

"Yep. Letting someone leave hungry or without a to-go container is not how they like things to work out. They'll stuff you full. If you're overwhelmed, do not look outside."

"Why?" I crane my neck to do, in fact, what he said I shouldn't.

"Dessert options are just as bad. Look like s'mores are on the agenda for tonight."

"I love s'mores."

He snorts. "When have you ever made s'mores?"

"With Grace."

"But you've never been camping?"

"Nope."

He studies me for a moment and then nods to a set of patio doors. "Let's go outside."

There are two places open for us at the table, so I take a seat and note how Lexi lays on a lounger with a book by the pool, two other smaller girls are occupied on the shallow end of the pool, and the tiniest one is in his mom's arms.

"Come check this out," Ben says, waving Graham over. He winks at me, and then they both disappear behind the guesthouse.

I'd been nervous five minutes ago, but the vibe of his entire family is just as relaxing as when I'm alone with Graham. When these three weeks are up, he better watch out. I might not want to—why is his sister staring at me and smiling like she knows something I don't?

"How is the road trip going?" she asks. The baby starts to fuss, so she rocks side to side.

"Good. I'm not sure how much he told you."

"Basically, all of it. When he said you were coming with him, I sort of forced it out of him."

"I'd have done the same if it were my brother."

"Have you crossed anything off the list yet?"

"We rode a roller coaster today."

She stops rocking, and her eyes go wide.

"Graham went on a roller coaster?"

I nod.

"Willingly?"

I laugh. "Don't worry. He was full of regret and puked as he predicted."

His sister's head rolls back with a laugh.

The rest of the night revolves around easy conversation and watching the kids play. The best part, though, is when I finally hold the baby.

No-nanny motherhood is totally in the cards for me someday.

"I'll call about rooms for the hotel next week first thing in the morning."

I glance around the cutest guesthouse filled with yellow and white accents. I take note of the kitchen, bathroom, living room, and the single bedroom.

"It's fine. I keep telling you that."

He rubs his neck. "I still think you deserve some privacy and shouldn't be forced to share a room or whatever with me."

He's very persistent about this. I sort of wish he'd be the guy who says, yeah, we're adults and can share a bed, and then bam! We wake up cuddling and spooning and there's an accidental kiss or a finger rubs against the bare skin of my stomach, but nope. Just trusty old respectable Graham Wright making sure I get the privacy I deserve. Why does that make him even hotter? I need him to have a negative quality or something. Bring him down a notch.

"Fine. Then I'll take the couch this time."

He opens his mouth, but I cut him off.

"Don't argue. I've watched you twist and turn enough today to know your back hated it."

"Which is exactly why you're not sleeping on it."

Suddenly, all the lights to the main house turn off.

Graham holds up a finger.

"Let's table this discussion. First, are you ready to cross something else off your list?"

"Yes, but I don't recall any of them that can be done in a blackout."

He grins, and I follow his gaze to the pool.

"Oh, no, no, no."

"You said you wanted to skinny-dip. You didn't specify where."

"This is your sister's pool, Graham. No."

"Their rooms are on the other side. Just be quiet and no

one will know. Plus, this community is locked up with security. There are zero people trying to peek over the fence. It's private."

"What if your sister and brother-in-law come out and find me just swimming naked in their pool? What do I say?"

He smiles and licks his lips. "Bucket list, baby."

I guffaw and shake my head. "Come with me, then."

"What? No. I'm not skinny-dipping with you."

"Why? Because it's your sister's pool?"

"No, because we don't both need to be naked in the pool."

"Awww, afraid you won't be able to resist me?"

"Paige."

"Just come on, please."

He shakes his head, so I stick my lip out. "You're supposed to help me cross things off my list by doing them with me, remember?"

"I don't remember that part of the deal."

"I do. It's why you came with me today knowing you'd get sick."

"No, that was because I wasn't going to make you do something that made you nervous alone."

I shrug. "Same thing here."

His eyes lock on mine.

"Fine. But let me turn the pool lights off, right?"

"Deal."

He sneaks out the door. Once the pool lights are off, moonlight is all we have. It's the best I'm going to get.

"You go first," I say. "I'll wait here."

The look he gives me is wicked, but in a good way. Like he's just now processing that we'll both be naked.

The thought didn't slip my mind. Nope. I can't remember

the last time I've been this giddy around a guy I'm actually nervous about.

He strips his shirt, kicks his shoes off, and starts to unbuckle his pants.

"Are you going to watch?" he asks.

I spin around quickly. Talk about being in a daze. His body literally had me mesmerized.

I hear a slight splash and slowly turn around.

Okay, he's in the pool, and now it's my turn.

I can do this.

I can totally do this.

He smiles, winks, and then turns around to face the main house.

I strip quickly before I can change my mind, then slink into the water.

"Okay." Only my head is bobbing above the waterline.

Graham turns and smiles.

"Look at you."

On instinct, I cover my breasts, but his gaze never leaves mine.

"Another thing to cross off the list. At this rate, you'll run out of things to do."

"Doubtful."

He treads closer to me. "What do you want to cross off next?"

I try to mentally envision the list, but all my brain can process is that Graham is swimming closer to me. I move back a little, because right now, the look he's giving me is making my heart race. Kiss Graham Wright naked in a pool should be on my list. Kissing him in general should be on my list.

"What are you thinking?" I ask before he can get too close.

He doesn't have time to answer before the lights in the main house turn on. His body crashes into mine, pushing me back to the side of the pool. If anyone were to walk out here, I'd be covered completely.

On instinct, my legs brush against his, and my hands hold on to him around the neck.

He looks over his shoulder at the house, where his brother-in-law walks into the kitchen and grabs a bottle of water from the fridge. Just as quickly as he appears, he's gone. The lights, however, don't shut off right away.

I take a deep breath, and the movement captures Graham's attention. His eyes take in the closeness of our bodies before settling on mine. My lips twitch into a smile.

"I think he's gone now."

"I know he is."

"Okay."

"I …"

His eyes close, and his nose nudges against mine.

"Paige," he whispers.

"Yes." My leg starts to hook around his hip, and I feel him come to life between us.

He lets out a breath, and his hand touches my hip.

I've never been more ready for a kiss in my life. For more than a kiss.

Right here, with Graham. It feels right.

But all too suddenly, he jerks back and rubs a hand over his face.

"I'm sorry. That was … that …" He doesn't finish that sentence. "I'm getting out."

I turn before he can see the reaction on my face.

I won't cry, but it doesn't hurt any less to know that feeling was only one-sided.

CHAPTER FIFTEEN

GRAHAM

I'm the one who wanted something different. I'm the one who said I needed to step outside of my comfort zone if I wanted things to change.

And fuck, did I ever.

The last twenty-four hours have been brutal. Well, it's been great, but brutal in the fact that now that any time Paige passes by me, my body springs to life. To be more specific, a very singular part springs to life. Memories of her body flush against mine and the way her cheeks turned pink when I almost kissed her are all that I can focus on.

Fucking. Hell.

For a man who loves control, I've strayed so far from the damn path, I can't even fucking see it anymore.

For the record, I won the argument of who would sleep on the couch last night. It was me.

We stayed for breakfast but hit the road by lunch, which is great because I didn't get any writing done this morning. I was too focused on what I should or shouldn't say to Paige.

Turns out, not much. She slept the whole way back to Wind Valley and then I left for the coffee shop to write as soon as the bags were out of the car.

Do I want Paige? Yes. Do I wish we could be more? Yes. But as manly as I am, I still have a heart, and I'd prefer it if it didn't break. So there's no point in putting myself out there to get hurt. Plus, what happens if I make a move and then things don't work out? Would she tell her dad to pull my contract as quickly as she asked him to get one started? If he's going to get one started. She hasn't said, and now, after last night, I feel like a dick bringing it up.

I just have to trust that she's doing what she said she'd do just like I am by letting her join me on my road trips.

I pause my fingers over my keypad and glance up.

I'm over here mentally fighting between my thoughts of Paige and what's happening in this book in front of me, and people are just moving about Loves A Brewing with their normal day. Drinking their iced teas and hot coffees and Frappuccinos. Not a single one of them knows that I started to write a sexy scene just to clear my head of Paige. To be honest, maybe this is the direction I should take with all my writing. I mean, I'm good at it. I've let the burn build so perfectly that they're just now about to rip each other's clothes off, and it feels more real than it should.

I look back at my screen, lowering my headphones. I love listening to music while I write, but I'm about to get deep, so taking my headphones off feels like I'll be able to concentrate.

I push thoughts of Paige to the back of my head and skim the last sentence I wrote.

"I've wanted you since the day I met you," she whispers

into my ear as I slowly pull her panties down her leg. As soon as I drop them to the floor, she spreads her—

"Join hands and let us pray."

I snap my attention up to the table in front of me.

Sure as shit. They are heads down, eyes closed, hands together praying.

Then there is me, the guy writing a scene on his laptop where the hero is about to go down on his heroine who just opened her legs for him.

Does this mean I'm going to hell?

I start closing open apps on my screen because I'm convinced it helps me clear my mind. The app for my text messages pops up. Now I know that sometimes there can be a delay in how it cross-loads with my phone or iPad, but I don't remember the top conversations. In fact, it's … oh shit.

I know from just the first line that I should not read it, but I can't stop myself.

I think I scared him away.

Who?

Graham.

Oh, the sexy god man who whisked you away from my resort on your wedding day.

You can just call him Graham.

Boring. But do tell. How could you, of all people, scare him off?

Well, basically, last night he had every chance to kiss me, but he didn't take it.

I'll skip the details, but we were naked in a pool together and our bodies were touching, and he just bailed.

I close my eyes and shake my head. *Do not keep reading. Do not do it.*

You actually went skinny-dipping! I'm so proud of you.

Can we get back to the problem here?

You found a good guy, Paige. There is nothing wrong with that.

Yes, but it sucks. There is so much chemistry between us that I swear when we are in a room together, one of us is bound to snap.

Just kiss him and see what he does.

I can't do that. Last night he made it clear that is not what he wants.

Paige, this is the first guy I've heard you gush about in years. YEARS. You can't just push it to the side. This is huge.

> I know, but I don't know at the same time.
> Eventually, I have to go home. Do you think
> he'd be interested in a fling? Like a
> summer-only thing?

You won't know till you ask.

> Good point. Gosh, Grace, I wish you were
> here. You have to meet him.

> Maybe we can get away to the lodge one
> weekend. You'd love him.

> But only one of us gets to lick his abs at the
> end of the day, and I call dibs.

Damnit.

> I can't even describe how sexy this man is.
> Not only did he save me from making a
> huge mistake, I want to lick his entire body.

> I'd spend time in a few areas more than
> others, but wow, I have never felt like this
> about anyone before AND—

I snap my computer shut.

Oh shit.

Oh.

Shit.

I did not need to read that. No sir, I did not.

I'm not an idiot. I know who she's talking to. I, however, did not think that perhaps I would be able to read anything Paige and Grace talked about. Or all of it.

Fuck.

I need to delete the thread without reading any more of it. That's an invasion of privacy, and I will not do that to her. I've already read too much. I don't even care that this is my computer, and I should be able to read anything on it I want. Nope. I will not read that. Again.

I back my chair up a little and stare at the silver top of my Mac.

You're not going to look.

I shake my head.

She's been through enough with guys she can't trust. Don't be another one.

I shake my head again.

Nope. You don't need to act on what she said either. Not all feelings require action. Don't forget the consequences.

I stand quickly and pace behind my chair before heading for the cashier.

"Hey, Graham," Will greets me. Will is Beck's brother-in-law. Living in a smaller town like ours has its advantages. "Having a tough time with your current work in progress?"

I shake my head. "Something like that."

"What can I get you?"

"A shot of espresso."

"Coming right up. I'll bring it to you." I glance at my table and back at him.

"I'll wait here."

He grins. "Need a break from your characters?"

"More like need a break from myself."

His brows dip toward his nose. "Is there anything I can help you with?"

"Nope. Not unless you're an expert in how to be near a

woman and never ever tell her that you—" I pause and notice how intently he's waiting for me to go on. "Never mind."

He nods slowly. "Okay, so you don't want to talk about it. That's fine. Can you write about it?"

"Write about it?"

"Yeah, if you have something going on in real life that can't happen. Can it happen for your characters instead?"

I could write some of my hero actions based on what I'd do to Paige if we had met at another time. Not just the sexy parts, which I'd, of course, think of her, but the entire plot. I could do that. It would be like a form of therapy to keep me from doing something I shouldn't.

I nod, grabbing my shot. "Thanks for the chat. This will help with my newfound spark of motivation."

"Anytime. It's on the house."

I put the money I'd taken from my wallet to pay for my shit into the tip jar.

"That's not what I meant," Will says.

"Consider it a payment for the help."

I retreat to my seat before he can say more.

I open my computer, quickly exit the messaging app, open my Word document again, and get to work.

If I can't act on how I feel about her, the hero in my novel will.

And his happily ever after won't end with the heroine leaving the way mine will.

CHAPTER SIXTEEN

PAIGE

I've spent most of the day in my room. Or, well, Graham's spare room.

He left as soon as we got back, and I was okay with that. I'm a little embarrassed at how last night went. I can't even imagine what he must think of me. Girl leaves fiancé at the altar and then wants to join a stranger on a road trip, and a week later she's naked in a pool with him, totally ready to let him do whatever he wants to her.

I step out of the much-needed hot bath and dry off.

He must think I'm crazy, but I'm not. All it takes is one choice to live a totally different life. That's exactly what I did. There's nothing wrong with that.

The knock at my door startles me.

"Paige, I grabbed the mail on my way back and there's a box here from your brother."

I step out of my room, my towel the only thing covering my body, and meet Graham in the kitchen. I cross one arm over my chest and hold the towel in place.

"Thank you." I take the box from him.

I turn back to my room; the only noise behind me is something that sounds like a person blowing raspberries with their lips.

I stop and turn. Graham's heated gaze collides with mine.

"Are you okay?" I ask.

Instead of answering, his eyes take their slow and teasing time soaking every inch of my body. He's not touching me, but he might as well be with the way he's looking at me. Like I'm standing here completely naked instead of in a fluffy white towel. It makes my heart race, and a small part of me wants to drop the towel. Give him what he's clearly thinking about. But he's made it clear that no matter how attracted to me he is, he won't give in.

But boy oh boy, do I wish he would.

I could tease him more, flirt with him, make any sort of move that might break him, but I won't.

"Graham?" This time he snaps to attention.

"Yeah?" He instantly reaches back to rub his neck.

I can't even enjoy that he's conflicted about me. Now it makes me more sad than anything that he won't just let himself have what he wants.

"You're staring."

"Sorry." He shakes his head and turns for his room.

Once his door is closed, I let out a sigh.

I have never met a man with more strength than Graham Wright.

I grab a pair of scissors out of the drawer in the kitchen and retreat to my room as well. I'd open it out here, but if he decides to come out, I don't want to put him through more misery by having to look at me in a towel again.

Preston sent me a brand-new phone—I know this because it is a different color, and this is not the case that was on the one I left at the resort—with all my information already on it. Inside the box is a little clutch purse with cash and credit cards, a new ID, a bag of milk chocolate-covered almonds, and my favorite lip color.

If I lucked out anywhere in life, it was with my brother. My family isn't horrible, but he pays attention to detail the most, and these almonds, well, ever since my mom reminded me of the sugar in them, let's just say she never knows when I have them in the house.

That makes her sound awful, but honestly, the environment we grew up in is nothing but pressure. It has its perks, don't get me wrong, but the pressure is on a level I have not missed since I got to Graham's place.

I plug my phone in, send Preston a quick thank-you text, and ignore all the unread messages that pop up. Then I trade my towel for a pair of cut-off jean shorts and a white cropped scoop neck top. I braid my hair to the side, tugging it to make it look bigger and then slip my feet into a pair of white sneakers.

Adding just mascara and pale pink lip color, I grab the almonds and return to the kitchen.

Graham is back in his writing seat.

"Want to try these?" I ask and sit with him.

He glances up. His eyes move just as slowly as before, and somehow, I feel more exposed than when I was wearing just a towel.

I push the bag toward him.

How can someone make my heart race by just looking at me?

"These are my favorites," I add. "Try one."

He runs a hand over his face, a smile appearing.

"You're persistent. Are you trying to poison me?

I shake my head with a wide smile. "No, they're just the best. Melt-in-your-mouth perfect. You'll never taste anything as sweet and addicting."

He looks me dead in the eye and says, "I highly doubt that."

With my nipples on full alert, I stand quickly.

"I thought I'd go to the store today, actually pull my weight in groceries and household things now that I have my own money again."

"That's not necessary."

He says it calmly, his gaze back on the computer screen and his fingers tapping away.

I twist my mouth, wanting to say more, but I don't want to keep bugging him. So instead, I make myself an ice water and take a seat on the patio. Birds chirp and a light breeze touches my skin. I prop my feet up on the footstool and grab the pair of sunglasses on the table. Leaning back with my drink and almonds, I let out a breath.

Wow. This is a wild feeling. It's not my first time sitting out here, but the more I sit out here, the more I can't imagine being anywhere else. Someone in the building catty-corner from me walks out onto their patio. I jerk upright, ready to hide back in the house, but she simply waves and then sits with a tablet in her hands.

I wave back awkwardly, even though she isn't paying attention now, and slowly lean back again.

I'm starting to think this town might not care who I am. Now, I know she can't see me enough to make out who I am, but with the few run-ins that I have had with people here, they seem so private.

I glance back into the house, and like always, I can't help but smile when I see Graham. His life here is simple and quiet, and mine is anything but that. Even if something did happen between us, where would we go? How would we make it work? If my dad doesn't take his books, would he just shut me out?

No. Graham's heart is too good for that.

As if he senses me watching him, he looks up. He winks, and I turn back around.

A few moments later, the sliding door opens.

"Hey." Graham pokes his head outside. "Simon needs some plotting help. I'm going to head to his place for a bit. Are you good here?"

"Of course."

Is he avoiding me?

I sit outside for maybe twenty more minutes before I hear the front door open and quiet footsteps follow.

Did he come back to talk?

I rise quickly and step into the apartment.

"Paige," a woman whispers right before Graham's friend from the other day tiptoes her way in. She beams a smile when she sees me. "Okay, sweet. I wasn't going crazy."

I laugh. "Are you dropping off more artwork?"

"I was actually coming here to see if you want to sneak out."

"Sneak out?"

She nods. "Well, yeah. I assumed you were out of town with Graham, but now you're here, and I thought it might be nice to hang out with someone other than him for a bit."

That sounds really nice right now.

"So I brought this." She holds up a wig, a hat, and sunglasses.

I burst into laughter.

"Is it that bad?"

I shake my head. "No, it's perfect. I'll just take the hat and glasses, though."

"You're coming?"

I shrug. "Why not?"

Making rash choices has been my thing lately, and why would this be any different? The whole point of the list is to find myself. I'm sure this choice will fit right in.

"Where are we headed?" I ask.

"To a nutrition studio," she says as if I should have already known.

"Wow. We're getting super wild, aren't we?"

She grins over her shoulder. "One of my best friends owns it. My other best friend works with her, so really, it's a girls' lunch, because they are hard workers."

"And you're not?"

"No, I am. I just have a schedule that lets me be anywhere I want at any time, and right now, I'm getting you out of this condo for the afternoon."

I smile at the joy on her face.

"Let's do it."

Our drive is short. That's one of the things I love most about Wind Valley so far. It doesn't take long to get anywhere.

It's a little like déjà vu as I walk into the studio. The two women Calla has claimed to be her best friends stare at me. They blink and they breathe, but their mouths are slightly agape.

"I … am I looking at what you're looking at?" One nudges the other's arm.

"Are you looking at Calla, who is standing right next to Paige King?"

"You did say Paige King, right?"

"Oh, stop it, guys. She's totally normal." Calla walks right in and sets down the bags of food we picked up on the way here. She starts to unpack them at a small round table for four in the back of the studio, so I move to help her.

"Will your friends be okay?" I ask.

"Yeah, totally. Yesterday was a hot topic on where the famous Paige King might be. Not once did I say I actually knew where you were, so they might be in shock."

"Did you plan that?"

"Wait, you knew where she was?" one of them asks, then she turns to me. "Hi, I'm Willa. And this is Greer."

Greer waves.

"I did know, but I promised her I wouldn't tell anyone."

"Not even Beck?" Greer snorts.

"Nope."

Will and Greer laugh.

"Let me get this right." Willa crosses her arms. "You kept a secret from Beck, and you've been hanging out with Paige?"

"Not hanging out per se," I cut in. "Just when she pops into Graham's place for interior stuff. It's a given."

"Graham's place?" Greer asks. "You're … you're staying with Graham?"

I nod. "Well, we just got back from a weekend road trip, but yes."

Willa sits down, and Greer pinches the spot between her

eyes. "Okay, we need food, and then we need all the details you can or want to give us."

I sit at the table as Calla slides me my take-out box. "It's, um, a short story really. I met him at the lodge on the weekend of my wedding, and then when I saw him leaving the morning of, I sort of just … went with him."

"So you just got in a total stranger's car and followed him home?" Willa asks, ignoring her friends. She isn't asking to be mean. Her tone is soft enough that I think she's just processing what I said out loud.

"Yes, I did."

Greer sits next to me and grabs a box for herself. "Well, if she was going to pick any of the guys, Graham is probably the safest."

"Between him, Tobias, and Simon." Willa volleys her head. "Simon is nice too."

"Simon is grumpy, Willa," Greer says and then smiles at Calla. "Sorry."

"Don't apologize to me. I grew up with him. He is grumpy. Simon is my brother."

"Wait, your brother is Simon Stone?"

She nods.

I hold up my hand.

"When you say *the guys*, are you referring to Graham's writing group?"

They nod.

"I'm engaged to Zane." Willa beams and shows me her hand.

"Oh my gosh, congratulations. You must be the ones who got engaged at the lodge."

"We are."

Conversation falls easy and thankfully away from me. I listen to them talk about their plans for weddings, work, trips, and the summer. It seems it's book signing season, and even though Graham has told me a bit about them, there's more travel involved than I would have thought.

"Is this all boring to you?" Calla asks me.

"Not at all. I actually like it."

I love listening to them plan their lives. Not have them planned for them.

"But it's probably a lot less cool than dressing up for big events and red carpets and glam stuff."

"I do enjoy that, but it's not as cracked up as they make it look. Pictures and real life are not the same."

"Oh jeez," Willa says and laughs. "You have spent so much time with Graham, you're starting to sound like him."

"How?"

"He hates social media or anything that talks about him without him knowing about it first."

"But he has accounts for his books, right?"

"He controls them completely," Calla adds. "He pays our friend Nora to manage them, but he creates every single post, and he never shows his face."

"Ever?" I ask. It seems dumb to ask, since he's made it clear to me how he feels, but I'm constantly surrounded by people who love having their picture taken. It feels normal to me at this point.

Calla nods.

"Do you know why?"

They all share a look, but the response isn't the one I was expecting.

"He's just always been a private person. It honestly surprises me that he writes under his real name," Calla says.

My phone buzzes, and all eyes fall to the screen.

"Holy crap, look at all those red dots," Greer says, covering her eyes. "Put it away or my anxiety will spike, and it's not even my phone."

I laugh. "Yeah, I've been meaning to look at my texts. I just got my phone back this morning and have been avoiding it."

The girls start to discuss the upcoming weekend. I'll be gone with Graham again, but it's all so … homey. I'm told when and where to be in my world, but not these girls.

I'm starting to think that that's not really the life I want anymore.

CHAPTER SEVENTEEN
GRAHAM

As soon as I walked in the door to complete silence, I knew something was different.

I won't panic. Paige can take care of herself, but in moments like this, living in a condo where you can cover the entire square footage of the place in less than a minute is nice.

Not finding Paige anywhere—not nice.

I have no way to reach her, and I … her phone! She has a phone now, but I don't know her number. Hell, I should have asked for it before I left earlier today. I can never think straight when I'm around her, so it makes sense that the simple thought slipped, but right now I really wish I could get my shit together when it comes to Paige.

All right, Graham, think.

This morning she said she wanted to go to the grocery store. I look at the clock on the stove. It's almost 6:00 p.m. Would she be there now? Maybe she waited for the evening so there would be fewer people?

She doesn't know anyone here, so it's not like she—

Calla!

Fuck. I don't know Calla's number either. I could call Beck, but then I'd have some explaining to do.

I let out a breath. She's an adult. I'll give her an hour, and then I'll worry. If she decides to leave, that's her choice and I'll respect it, but … damn it.

If she's gone …

If I never took the chance …

Fuck.

I rub my hand over my face and sit on the couch. I wanted to do the right thing. I wanted to be the person she needed after she walked out on her wedding. I wanted her to know she could trust me to just be there for her, not be this random guy she met at a hotel who wants to strip her clothes off and kiss every single soft inch of her body just because they are spending twenty-four-seven together.

I …

As soon as I hear a key at the door, I jump from the couch and rush to it. I'm swinging the door open before whoever on the other side has a chance to do it.

Paige's green eyes meet mine and a soft smile touches her lips. A sense of calm courses through my body. I pull her to me quickly, wrapping my arms around her as hard as I can.

"Whoa, I can't breathe." She taps my shoulder.

"Awww."

My moment of peace is interrupted as my gaze finds Calla.

"You missed her." She points at me and winks.

I let go of Paige and step back. "I was worried."

"Clearly." Calla snorts.

"I, uh," I rub the back of my neck. "I wasn't aware that

you were going out today with Calla." I let my gaze fall back to Paige, who hasn't taken her eyes off me since I hugged her.

Okay, yeah, so we don't hug a lot, but damn it, the fear that ran through me when she wasn't here, I can't even explain. I thought I wasn't going to see her again.

I don't like the thought of that.

"Oh shit," Calla says and wrinkles her face. "That's right." She starts to back up slowly. "I'm not here. I'm leaving."

"Wait," I call out as she stumbles. "Are you drunk?"

She presses her lips together and shakes her head. "Tipsy-ish. I'm a lightweight. It was like three glasses of wine."

I pin a glare toward Paige.

It's not even dark yet. Were they both day drinking? That's fine, but how did they get back here?

"Oh," Paige says and then digs in her coat pocket. "Your keys. Right. I drove."

"No fucking way," I say and grab the keys before Calla can.

"I wasn't going to give them to her," Paige says. "I was just pointing out that she can't go anywhere since I had them."

I look at Calla. "I'll drive you home."

"Oh shit," Calla says again, and Paige lets out a laugh.

Paige holds her hands up. "I didn't drink at all, I swear. This is all just funny."

"It's not funny. Coming home to find my place empty and not having any idea where you were is not funny. Hell, I thought you left and that I'd never—"

"Calla!"

I close my eyes at the new voice.

Beck. What the hell is he doing here? *Picking up Calla, duh.*

"Oh, yeah, soooo…" Calla starts. "I texted Beck to pick me up from your place. I'm just now putting it together how it looks and how—" She pauses to point at me and then at Paige. "We can't lie now."

Beck's mouth is open, ready to ask questions, then he spots our little trio outside my door. He looks from one of us to the other, crosses his arms with a smirk, and nods.

"This makes so much sense right now." He holds out his hand. "Beck Robertson."

"Paige King."

He starts to chuckle. "You know," he begins and places his arms around Calla's shoulders to pull her closer to him, "I knew you didn't buy that girl's stuff online for your sister, but this was not what I expected."

"What did you expect?" Paige asks without missing a beat.

"Don't answer that," I say just as quickly.

I need to get ahold of this situation, and I need to do it fast.

"You"—I point to Calla— "need water and food. You"—I point to Beck— "need to get her home and keep this to yourself until Paige says otherwise. And you"—I point to Paige— "need to get inside before any more people in this town spot you."

She waves at Calla. "I had a great time this afternoon. Thank you."

"You were gone all afternoon?" I ask.

"God, you are fucking cute," Calla says.

"Go," I order my best friend and his wife.

"You're going to fill me in once we're in the car, right?" Beck asks as they head down the steps.

"Oh, totally."

I roll my eyes and follow Paige inside my place.

"I'm sorry I wasn't here when you got home and that I didn't leave a note. I honestly thought you'd be happy to have an empty place for an hour or two. In hindsight, yeah, I probably should have found a way to reach out."

Well, she pretty much just covered it all. Brains, beauty, and she's great at communicating. Fuck. She's the perfect woman.

I grab my phone from my back pocket. "What's your number?"

Paige laughs, but when she sees the look in my eyes, she stops and recites it quickly.

"Thank you," I say and step around her. I'm not even sure where I'm going, but there are too many emotions for me to process right now.

I'm normally a laid-back guy, but whatever just happened has agitated me.

"Graham, I'm sorry. I should have left my number or called you or asked to call or—"

"You don't have to be sorry." I toss my hands up. "I just didn't like coming home and not having you here."

My hands drop to my side at my admission.

That might have been too much. We both know this isn't forever, so eventually me coming home and her not being here is a given. I'm acting out of line for whatever this is between us.

"In the hall, Beck cut you off. What were you going to say?"

I shake my head. If I think my last statement was too

much, finishing that one is going to scare her right back to Calla.

"Nothing."

"Tell me." Paige steps closer.

I step back but don't look away.

"Nothing. Just as I said. I don't like coming here and not finding you."

"No … I think you were saying something else."

"Nope."

I bump into the wall, but it doesn't stop her. She takes one more step and reaches out, her hand cupping my cheek to force me to look at her. "You were going to say that you were worried you'd never see me again, weren't you?"

She's tempting me on purpose. She wants to play this game? It's like playing with fire. We both know how this will end, and yet she's not stopping.

Fine. I can play too.

I let my hands fall to my hips and tug her closer.

Then I spin to push her back against the wall.

"Yes. The thought of never hearing your voice or seeing your smile again kills me."

Her breathing picks up, and her gaze drops to my lips.

She's so close. Just one inch, maybe two, and our lips would be touching. I'd be kissing her. Holding her. She'd be kissing me and pressing her body against mine. Just like last night in the pool. God, I wanted her then. Right now, I think I want her more.

My jeans are growing tight.

I want it so badly, but we can't. She's only here temporarily and only because she wants my help. At some point, she will go home.

Still, I can smell the vanilla shampoo and the citrusy lotion she's been using. It does things to me that I never thought a smell could do.

"Paige." I breathe as her nose touches mine.

This is a bad idea, but hell, thinking she left without me knowing how it feels to have her feels wrong too.

"Yes."

How to describe my feelings are on the tip of my tongue, but as a man who has always been a fan of actions speaking louder than words, I choose to show her instead.

I nudge my knee between hers and press into her. She gasps; I capture her lips with mine.

I knew they'd be soft. I knew they'd be plump. God, they feel so fucking perfect against mine.

A small moan escapes her as she tugs my hair.

Hell, I had no idea I'd like my hair being pulled, but I fucking love it.

I press into her harder. My growing erection pushes against her stomach as my tongue swoops into her mouth.

And she tastes like cinnamon. Spicy and hot, and I'll never smell or taste it again without thinking of Paige in my arms as I kiss her with all that I have.

As her hands continue massaging my head, I move my right hand to the back of her thigh and the other slides around her hip to cup her butt.

With a small jerk, I lift her slightly and angle her until my hard-on is pressed perfectly between her legs.

"Oh, fuck, Graham," she breathes, breaking the kiss to give me access to her neck. "This is better than I imagined."

I kiss her collarbone. "I couldn't agree more."

I unbuckle my belt and do the same for her. She shimmies

out of her shorts quickly, and as soon as she's done, I put her right back in the same position, only this time, the hand that had been holding her leg moves between them.

"How much do you want this?" I ask, pulling her earlobe into my mouth and then kissing her lips hard.

She bites my lip. Then she grabs my hand and guides me to the spot between her legs where she wants me most.

"You tell me," she says.

I waste no time moving her underwear to the side and sliding two fingers in.

"Hell, Paige, you're soaking wet."

"Can you blame me? The tension between us has been so thick that as soon as you touched me, my body had no choice but to obey."

"Obey," I repeat and pull back. "I like the sound of that."

"So do it. I'll do anything you want."

"Anything?"

"Yes." She moans as my free hand joins the other, rubbing her clit.

"I'll remember that, but right now … right now I just want to watch you get off on my fingers as you say my name. I want you to be reminded of how a man should treat you. Of how a man should always put you first."

I press my mouth to hers before she can say anything. Both hands move faster until she's writhing in my arms. She breaks our kiss, her breathing frantic.

"Oh god. Oh god. Oh god."

"Move your hips, baby. Take what you want. Show me what you want."

Her body doesn't hesitate, and I just about release in my pants at her response.

"Take it. Take it, baby. That's right. Ride my fingers."

"Oh shit!" she screams as she clamps around my fingers, folding forward and biting my shoulder.

Her chest is heaving as she looks up, a glow on her face. "Wow."

You're telling me. There is no way in hell I'll be able to keep my hands to myself now.

If I thought I wanted Paige before she just fell apart in my arms, I was wrong. I just hit a whole new level. What just happened is only the beginning, and no matter how many times I tell myself that it can't happen again, if she makes a move, I'm not sure I have the self-control to stop it.

CHAPTER EIGHTEEN

PAIGE

Holy shit.

Those two simple words have played on repeat since last night.

Holy shit.

I sit up higher on my bed, my back against the headboard as I turn the page to another one of Graham's books.

That man writes the steamiest slow burn sweet romances I've ever read. Like, you don't get the sex, but everything that happens up until they close the door, wow.

I fan myself.

It's probably best that he doesn't write sexy scenes.

Either way, if he wrote anything nearly close to what happened against the wall of his living room last night, girls would fall in love with him as quickly as ice cream melts in the sun.

Holy shit.

I grab my phone and thumb out a quick text to Grace. It's

a long overdue text now that my mind has had time to simmer on my actions.

> Something happened with Graham last night.

Are you okay? Why don't you call me?

> Because he's writing in the kitchen, and I don't want him to hear me.

You said he wears headphones when he writes.

> He might take them off.

I repeat, is everything okay?

> Physically ... better than okay. Mentally ... I'm not quite sure.

I'm just calling you.

"Grace," I answer the phone in a whisper. "He kissed me. He more than kissed me. We more than kissed. We didn't have sex, but oh my god, I've never crumbled like that for someone."

She laughs lightly. "Finally. God, Vincent was such a fucking tool. I mean, his whole no sex before the wedding thing he started a few months ago makes sense now, but even then, you never once talked about it."

It wasn't anything to talk about. Graham is different.

I let out a sigh. As much as I want to gush over what happened with Graham and how much I want it to happen again, I need to get back to the reason I reached out to her in the first place.

"We made a deal that if he helped me with a bucket list, I'd message my dad to publish his books with Vans."

"What?" She sounds like a mother whose child just talked back to her.

"I know."

"But you don't have anything to do with Vans. How can you convince your dad to do that? And you know how much your dad hates when people use their connections to get ahead. He likes people who put in the work and—"

On a groan I say, "I know. I know. I just … honestly didn't think I'd see Graham again after he helped me. I didn't think he mattered. I know how that makes me sound, but I just needed to get away, and I was so desperate that I made a deal that I … the chances of me holding up my end are slim."

"Extra fucking slim."

"Grace, help me."

"Okay, let's back up. The morning of your wedding, you came to me and told me all about this amazing guy you met the night before. Then you get in his car and follow him home, and somewhere in all that, your brain thought you'd never see him again. How is that possible? You were so giddy over him that morning."

"I don't know. It all happened so fast. Vince had just confessed to cheating, and bam! There is this super sweet guy just handed to me. Maybe I overread that night we had. Finding out you've been cheated on doesn't make you feel good, so maybe I—"

"I'm going to stop you right there. Whatever happened has happened, and clearly, after last night, there is something there. So now what are you going to do?"

I blow out a breath. "Call my dad and apologize for the wedding."

"Wait? You still haven't called him?

"No."

"Paige! You're not helping yourself."

"I know. I know. But he knows I'm okay." I sigh. "I'm a mess. Two weeks ago, my entire life was planned for me. Now, I've gone through so many emotions, and I've made a lot of rash choices since I jumped in his car, but I know I don't want to be someone who can't keep their word."

"Then don't. Call your dad. Grovel. He's probably upset with you, but you're his only daughter. It won't last long."

"Yeah."

"But don't come right out and ask about Graham in this first phone call. That might hurt you more than you think."

"I know, but the longer I—"

A knock at my door startles me.

"Paige, are you okay?" The door slowly opens, then Graham peeks in. He smiles immediately when he sees me. "Hi."

And then he has the audacity to blush a bit.

"Hi," I say back. "Grace, can I call you later?"

"You better. Good luck."

I hang up and set my phone down, standing to move and open the door wider.

"Is everything okay?" he asks again.

I nod. "Why wouldn't it be?"

Oh God. Did he hear me talking to Grace?

"You've been hiding in here most of the day." He rubs his neck. "Did I take things too far last night?"

"No, god no," I breathe out all too quickly, and he chuckles. "I mean, no. Last night was amazing."

"Okay."

If he's waiting for me to explain why I'm hiding in here, I won't. It's a blend between when I should call my dad and the fact that last night in no way means I can just kiss Graham or touch him whenever I want.

"If you're not busy"—he jerks his thumb over his shoulder— "I have something I want to show you."

"What is it?" I ask just as his hand grazes the small of my back as he guides me to the balcony.

He does, however, stop right before we reach the door. "Go check it out."

I give him a "what are you up to?" look and then peek out the doors. I see it instantly. Three medium-sized pots, a bag of soil, and a bunch of flowers.

"It's not a garden like you have on your list. I don't exactly have the space, but they are plants, and you still have to plant them, so maybe it can count."

"It definitely counts!" I say and leap into him to hug him tight. "It's perfect."

He laughs and hugs me back. "Okay, but don't ask me to help, because there's a reason all the plants in my place are fake."

I pull back, leaving my arms around his neck. "But you could sit out with me while I do it, right?"

His gaze settles on my lips, and instead of answering, his throat bobs as he nods.

"Great."

I wish he'd kiss me. I mean, come on, this is a kiss-worthy moment, isn't it?

He clears his throat and steps back.

"I'll bring my computer out here."

And then he's gone. He moves to the kitchen table while I step outside to attend to my new little garden.

I'm dumping soil into each pot when he comes back.

"I got you something else."

I set the bag down, sit back on my heels, and peek over my shoulder. What could he possibly have now?

My lips split into a wide grin when I see what he's holding up.

"Wow," I say and stand. "You're just pulling out all the stops, aren't you?"

I grab the stack of small paper squares from his right hand. "Do I do them all?"

"No, you just pick one, and then I'll bring out a damp towel. We press it to your skin and a minute later, viola, you have a tattoo."

"And it just washes off?"

"Yep. I figure you could try a couple, and if you really do like it, then you can go get a real one."

Oh my god. This man is just … wow. This is super thoughtful.

"Okay, let's do this one," I say to the one that's three black hearts.

He meets me in the living room with a damp towel.

"Where do you want it?" he asks.

"Right here," I say and pull my shirt to the left a little to expose my collarbone.

His eyes flash from the spot just above my breast to my eyes.

"There?"

I nod.

He takes a breath and hands me the towel. "Well, there you go. Just peel it and press it and you are done."

I laugh.

"You can stick your fingers inside me and let me ride them till I climax, but you can't hold a towel to my chest for a single minute?"

Oh shit. Shit. Where did that come from?

His gaze turns heated.

"It wouldn't just be a minute, Paige."

"Ah, well then, maybe you shouldn't keep doing all these things for me that put you in this kind of position."

I expect him to have a quick-witted response like before, but he thinks for a moment and says, "Well, you're only here a few more weeks, so I figure I'd hold up my end of the deal and help you cross as many things off this list as possible. So situations like this are inevitable."

And just like that, he brings me right back to reality.

The deal. How he's only doing these things to help me and not because he genuinely wants to do them. I know that's why, but a part of me thinks that even if the deal weren't a thing, he'd do them. I like to think that anyway.

He peels the sticker back and presses the small design to my skin. I wish I could say that his words had squashed the feelings his touch brings out in me, but they didn't.

My fingers still itch to touch him, and my body still craves to be flush against his. I still want to taste him and kiss him. I want him to thread his hands through my hair and hold me tight. I want him to not want anything other than me.

"Paige, you have to stop looking at me like that."

"Like what?"

"Like … like I have permission to do anything I want to you."

I'm not oblivious, okay? My bucket list is boring. As I've said, a thrill seeker is not who I am, but someone who doesn't go after what she wants … I don't want to be that woman.

"You do, and … I think you should kiss me. Right now. Kiss me. Touch me. Do whatever you want to me."

I'll worry about our deal and the consequences later. Right now, I just want Graham.

The towel falls to the floor, and he's whipping my shirt over my head in seconds. He smiles when he sees the three hearts, then he's tugging my bra to the side and pulling my nipple into his mouth.

He goes from zero to a hundred when he sees something he wants, and right now, I'm the fuel.

I let out a moan, because how could I not with his mouth on me? He pulls his lips away, squats with his hands behind my thighs, and stands, wrapping my legs around him.

He drops back onto the couch so that I'm straddling him and then cups my face, pulling my lips to his and stripping me of my bra.

We kiss like the building is on fire and if we don't move fast enough, everything will be lost.

"Fuck, Paige. How do you do this to me?"

He peppers kisses down my neck to my chest.

"I don't know, but the feeling is mutual."

He captures my mouth with his again. "Let's move to my room. Condoms are in the dresser next to my bed."

I nod quickly and climb off him, but he tugs me back, placing my legs back where they were so he can walk me himself as we kiss down the hall.

"I said go to my room—I didn't say stop kissing me."

I giggle against his mouth, but I follow orders. I kiss him hard and grind my hips against him.

"Fuck," he says, and the next words on his lips are stalled by a knock at the door.

"Ignore it," I say. "Kiss me again."

The knocks get louder.

He groans rather loudly and places me on my feet.

"It's Wednesday. The guys are here to write. Fuck. I forgot."

"You forgot they were coming over?"

He nods. "I made them switch last week when you were here and totally spaced this one."

"Graham, I need to piss, so I'm coming in!"

Graham rushes me backward into his room.

"Wait here. I'll try to get rid of them without looking suspicious."

I nod and pull my phone from my back pocket. "Don't rush. I have a few calls to make. I'll be quiet."

He nods, hesitating in the doorway, and then closes it.

I hover my thumb over my screen. Should call my dad or call Grace back? Then I look down.

My shirt and bra are both in the living room.

Shit.

CHAPTER NINETEEN
GRAHAM

Everyone is happy and content and ready to write for the afternoon.

Everyone but me.

I'm just sitting here, arms crossed with a stern gaze locked on my bedroom door.

Go figure. The two of us finally decide that we're going for it, consequences be damned, and my friends show up. For a group of guys who surround their entire lives with romance, they sort of suck right now.

Would the guys notice if I ducked in there for ten minutes and then came back?

Better yet …

I fake cough and everyone looks at me.

"Graham, what's your deal?" Zane asks.

"Huh?"

"Yeah, you're giving off weird vibes," Hero adds with a pull-it-together glare. "We've been here for like ten minutes, and you're just being weird."

Yeah, and for ten minutes they've ignored all my suggestions to head to the coffee shop to write today. Instead, they unpacked and set up their laptops at my kitchen table.

"And the look on your face is weird too." This coming from Simon. "Did you buy your sister's thongs again? I'd make that face too."

Tobias chuckles behind his hand, so I slap the back of his head.

"Stop. No. I didn't."

"So what is it? Why are you being weird?"

"I'm not being weird."

"You are."

"I'm not. There is nothing weird happening."

The sound of very obvious water running from inside my apartment fills the silence.

I don't think a single person at the table catches how wide my eyes go at the noise. Nope, they all turn to look at my bedroom door.

"Did someone just flush the toilet in your bedroom?" Zane asks.

"Is someone here?" Simon says at the same time.

"That's fucking weird, Graham."

Ignoring all of them, I stand.

"Excuse me," I say and stalk to my room just as the water shuts off and a loud commotion comes from inside. I rush into the room, feeling the energy of five bodies behind me as I swing the bathroom door open.

"Jesus, Paige! Are you okay?"

I reach out to help her up, her arms locking around me.

"I wasn't thinking when I flushed the toilet. I just put a shirt on and then came in here to wash—"

A throat clears, and we both snap our attention to the doorway. To the five heads filling the space to get a view.

Oh, hell.

Paige waves, shyly. "Hi."

Not one of them replies.

This time, I clear my throat.

"Guys, this is Paige. Paige, this is Zane, Beck, Simon, Hero, and Tobias."

They all speak at once.

"Hi."

"Hello."

"Hey."

"Holy shit," comes from Tobias at the end. "Paige King."

"Don't do that," I say, cringing.

"It's just Paige," she adds.

My gaze lands on Beck, the only one who hasn't said anything.

"It's good to see you again, Beck," Paige says and reaches her hand out. "And to officially meet you. Calla thinks the world of you."

"You knew she was here?" Tobias asks.

"We don't keep secrets and—"

"Stop talking," Simon says and pinches the bridge between his eyes. "Please."

Paige smiles, her teeth pulling her bottom lip into her mouth as she does.

Silence fills the bathroom.

"Should we get back to writing?" I ask and place my hand on Paige's lower back to move her out of the room where all my friends are now just staring at her.

Tobias guffaws. "Yah, like we can focus on writing when we have questions."

"So many questions," adds Hero.

I'm pretty sure Tobias is about to pop a blood vessel near his eyes. "Paige King," he repeats.

"It's just Paige."

"I—" He makes a mind-blowing gesture with his hands and walks out of the room.

"Good, yes, let's all go."

"This is just nuts," Zane says. "When did this happen?"

"How did this happen?"

"Does anyone know you're here?"

Paige looks at me, her slightly pink, as her eyes ask me how much we should tell them.

I shrug. That's her call.

"A little over a week ago. We met the weekend you got engaged." She points at Zane.

"You met that weekend!"

"She's right here, man, you don't have to yell."

"I'm sorry, but this is exciting," Zane says. "This is like the most exciting thing to ever happen in your life.

"Hey, I take offense to that," I shoot back.

"It's true," Beck says.

I fake hurt, but all in all, they're right.

Paige is just a smiling fool next to me. If they think my life is exciting over the sole fact that this woman is living with me, wait till they find out what else we've been up to. Or were about to be anyway.

"Wait a sec," Simon says as, finally, they all reclaim their spots at the kitchen table. He points to my room, to the guest room, and back to mine. "She was hiding in your room."

Oh shit. He's about to figure this out.

"And she's in your shirt."

"So?"

I try to play it cool and move to my spot at the table. I kid you not, you could hear a pin drop.

Everyone is staring at me now, including Paige.

In fact, it's her who breaks the silence with a *tsk*. "And you thought him having a temporary roommate was exciting. I guess he just hit a whole new record."

And with that, she grabs my face and kisses me right in front of everyone. Then she moves to the couch, grabbing her bra and the shirt I'd tossed to the floor earlier.

"I'm going to go call Calla. I'm pretty sure I need a girl's night and a drink after all that."

Paige waves to the table. "It was nice to officially meet everyone. I'm sure I'll see you again now that the cat is out of the bag."

No one says a word as she heads for her room and closes the door.

"So, who needs plot help?" I flash a cocky grin at the group.

Simon speaks first.

"I think I speak for all of us when I say please, *please* start from the beginning."

"Do not miss a single detail. Her name has been all over the internet. How the hell did this happen?"

For a split second, I debate not telling them everything, but the six of us have known each other for more than a decade. They would call bullshit in a heartbeat, and honestly, at this point, maybe it's best they know. I need someone to talk this out with.

So, I tell them everything up until this point, minus some of the steamier details.

"Fuck," Tobias says with a laugh. "You two are like a walking romance novel. Did she talk to her dad yet?"

"This could get complicated," Simon says. "It's wild, but I can see why you didn't tell anyone."

"So is she staying here for good now or what?" Hero asks.

"Just for a couple more weeks. Eventually, she'll go home. She can't just walk away from her life."

"Why not?" Beck asks. Of course, he would be the one to ask that.

"Our lives are too different."

"That's a stupid answer."

"Are you two … you know … more than friendly?" Zane asks. "Also, if Calla knows, does Willa know?"

"All the girls know," I say with a chuckle. "That night you picked up Calla"—I glance at Beck— "they were all together."

Zane laughs. "Ah, that makes sense. I went to pick up Willa from the studio one night, and she couldn't tell me why, but she said it was a day she'll never forget."

"Yeah, I guess Paige hasn't been hiding as much as she originally planned. And technically, a few people know where she is, so missing isn't exactly the word I'd use."

"Maybe she's just saying that she wants to hide out because she doesn't want to leave you."

Beck's words hit me right in the chest. That thought has crossed my mind, too, but it just … I don't see it working out that way.

"She had an entire life before me. It would be crazy for her to stay here."

"Hold on," Tobias cuts in and leans forward. "I'm still waiting on the answer from Zane's first question, because honestly, I've never seen you even show an ounce of interest in a woman. You've been a very private person since the day I met you, and now you pick *the* Forbes Princess as the one."

That pretty much sums up why we can't be together. The life she wants and the life I want aren't the same. But while she's here, we can make the most of it.

Everything will be fine.

CHAPTER TWENTY

PAIGE

Calla picked me up as soon as I called her. She said that the moment Beck told her he was headed to meet the guys at Graham's place, she had a feeling the guys would find out today.

"I wish I had been in the room when it happened." Willa laughs.

I sip my mojito and grab a nacho off the plate in front of us. Back home, I have friends, but not ones who are ready to just hang out after a spur-of-the-moment phone call.

Everything is so different when it comes to Graham and his friends.

I like it here. I like them.

"For a group of men who use words to pay their bills, they were all speechless," I say.

"I say that to Hero all the time."

"Same with Beck."

"Zane is exactly the same."

"I never say it, because I'm the only one here not dating a romance writer."

"Yet," Calla points the tip of her drink at Greer.

Greer rolls her eyes.

"Do you have a crush on someone?" I ask.

All the girls start talking at once, but Calla shushes them all. "She says she doesn't, but time will tell. The real question is, now that the guys know about you and we're clearly out in public, does this mean we can see you more?"

I nod. "Definitely."

To be honest, since the moment we walked into The Black Alcove bar, only three people have come up to ask if I'm Paige King. Others have simply waved in passing. It's nice, and it makes me feel a little guilty that I judged this town so quickly. Or most of the world too quickly. Fame isn't something they dwell on here. I could get used to it. If I never left.

But that's crazy talk.

I swirl my straw and listen to the girls. Willa is talking about how she'll be taking time off next year to plan the wedding, and since Greer is a one-on-one health coach, they'll need to hire someone to fill in.

I'd apply, but I know zilch about health. I've always just had someone tell me what to do. If I think about it, I've always had my own Greer.

"So how are things living with Graham?" Willa asks.

"What do you mean?"

All three girls share a look, but Calla is the one who speaks up.

"She means, how is living with a guy you met less than twenty-four hours before you moved in with him?"

"Oh, that." I laugh and then look at the stage where a band is setting up. "It's good."

More than good. Graham promised to text me as soon as the guys left, and I've been checking my phone, flipping it over on the table numerous times, as if I won't feel it vibrate with his message.

"She's got that smile," Willa says.

"She totally does," Greer adds.

"Something happened with Graham, didn't it?"

"What? No." My instant response just spurs them on even more.

"Lies."

"It totally did."

"Tell us. What's he like?" Calla asks.

"I bet he's the wildest of the bunch. He writes sweet romance, for crying out loud. That means he saves the real spicy stuff for the bedroom."

"Oh my gosh, you two stop. You're making her blush," Greer chimes in but smiles at me. "But they're right, aren't they?"

Let's face it, any mention of Graham and I'm smiling like a fool. "The past two weeks have been a whirlwind. He's pretty great. More than great."

"Oh god, we don't even have the juicy details and she's already got that look." Calla groans.

"What look?" Greer asks.

"The look that says something has happened, and she's smitten with him."

I laugh at that. "I leave in a couple of weeks. No matter how much fun we have, there is a timestamp."

"Booo. Says who?" Calla smacks the table. "You can stay!"

I won't lie, knowing others want me to stay, have even thought of it like I have, is nice.

"Maybe I'll visit" is how I answer.

I'm not sure if that will happen or if I'm just saying it because these women have welcomed me with open arms, but I'm adding spending more time in Wind Valley to my list as soon as I get home.

My phone buzzes just as Willa orders another round of drinks.

My heart starts to race, and I know I've got a big smile on my face when I flip it over.

But it's not a text from Graham. It's from Grace. Normally, I'd be happy about this, too, but the message displaying on my screen isn't one to smile about.

What did your Dad say?

With all the excitement of the afternoon, I forgot to call him.

I was so caught up in my day that I forgot to do something.

That's never happened to me before.

Being caught up in the moment, I mean. Being so into my life that I'm in the present without a care in the world.

Except I do. I care a lot. About Graham. More than a woman should over a man in just two weeks.

My phone buzzes again. This time it's from Graham.

. . .

> They're packing up. Should I come
> get you?

I type out a quick reply that I'll see him at home, and then I tell the girls I'll see them later. I try to give them cash, but they refuse it. That's also something I'm not used to.

The walk home takes me about twenty minutes, but it's the first time I've ever been able to say I walked home.

Wow.

I laugh at myself with each step up to Graham's apartment. I'm pleased by the smallest things. Who knew?

Mrs. Mason is standing outside when I make it to our floor. I've never actually seen her but given the way she's peeking out of her doorway; it's got to be her. She watches me carefully and then nods when I reach our shared floor.

"You're that girl, aren't you?"

"Excuse me?"

"The one in the magazines. The one who ran out on her own wedding."

"Oh, um …"

Graham's door opens before I can think of how to respond.

"Hey, what are you—oh, hi, Mrs. Mason. How are you tonight?"

"I'm well. Just speaking with your girlfriend here."

"Oh, I'm not his—"

"What are you asking her?" Graham asks.

"Oh, just saying hello. She's the girl from the magazine, right?"

Graham shakes his head with a smile. "Good night, Mrs. Mason."

He guides me inside with his hand on my lower back.

"Is she always this nosey?" I set my purse down. "I could have —"

Graham is swiftly pulling his shirt over his head. A flashback to the night we met hits me, and I don't even try to hide the wide smile I give him.

"Yeah," I nod. "Yes, okay. We're still on the same page. I'll just go change into something"—I wave my hand at my outfit— "less."

"Paige."

"Yeah?"

"Go to my room and take your clothes off."

For as much as I've complained about not wanting to be told what to do, I march my pretty little ass as fast as I can to his room.

I'll take orders from Graham Wright any time of day.

He stalks into the room, his presence invading my space enough to make me back up and bump into the bed.

I fall back, barely catching myself with my hands.

He leans over me, one knee on the bed outside of my right thigh while the other nudges my legs apart to rest between them. He leans forward, grips my chin gently to force me to look at him, and then presses his mouth to mine.

His tongue sweeps in, and he deepens the kiss.

Kissing Graham is my new favorite thing to do.

He crawls more on the bed, forcing me to lie on my back.

I don't resist. I want this more than he knows.

One of his hands moves to the button of my jean shorts. He flicks them open, unzips them, and then leans back to help me shimmy them off.

They get caught on my heel, and he growls.

I do this to him. I make him this crazy. I had no idea the control I would have over him, over anyone, and I love every moment of it.

My hands start to move just as frantically as his, and within minutes, we're both fully naked.

His hand glides up the inside of my legs as he resumes his position over me.

He kisses my chest, just above the tattoos he gave me earlier.

"That was the most brutal writing session of my life."

"Tell me about it," I say and tickle my hand down his stomach. "I've never checked my phone so many times for a text in my entire life."

His hand reaches the spot I crave him most, and he slides a finger in at the same time as he kisses me.

"Holy fuck, Paige, you're wet. Is this what I do to you?"

I pull his face back to mine so I can kiss him and bite his lower lip.

He adds a finger, curling them, and presses the heel of his hand against my clit. His hand moves so fast that I don't have time to prepare for the orgasm that rips through my body.

"Shit! Oh, shit!"

As if he wants to torture me with pure pleasure, he pulls his fingers out mid orgasm, rolls on a condom, and thrusts inside me.

"Fuck!"

"Shout ten swear words in less than thirty seconds" should

be on my list. Right there next to "have two orgasms in one night," because I know that's exactly where I'm headed. There might even be more.

I lift my hips to increase the pressure of each thrust. Graham grabs them and holds them up, his own hips relentlessly moving himself in and out at the perfect pace.

I'm about to have that number two when he pulls out, flips me over, lifts me to my knees, and pushes himself back into me.

Holt shit is on the tip of my tongue again. Sweet romance writer Graham Wright is blowing my mind right now. I expected soft, slow, intimate sex, not rough, I-can't-get-deep-enough-or- enough-of-you sex.

I'm completely shocked, but I'm absolutely here for it.

"Yes." I have the feeling that wild Graham wants to hear it. "Harder."

He groans but does as I say.

"Faster."

Again, he complies.

"Right there! Oh, fuck! Don't stop. Don't stop. Don't sto-o-o-o-op."

My vision goes fuzzy as my entire body forgets how to hold itself up. I close my eyes.

Graham captures my hips on a groan before collapsing on top of me.

"Jesus, Paige," he says between breaths.

I slowly roll to my side as he moves off me. We lay facing each other, chests heaving as we catch our breaths.

"We should do that again. After water."

He chuckles. "Oh, we're doing that again, and you can bet your ass that from this moment on, as long as you're here, you're mine. You're in my bed, and you're with me every-where I go."

He gets out of bed to clean himself up before I can reply.

Honestly, it's for the best. There's a war inside my brain between someone claiming me for the first time and the fact that no matter what happens between us, I'll be leaving.

I cover my face and take a breath.

For one day, maybe two, I'm going to pretend like this right here is the life I'll live forever.

CHAPTER TWENTY-ONE
GRAHAM

Two days. Two whole days I had Paige to myself. We spent most of it naked, but you won't hear me complaining. The only thing I have to complain about is the fact that we had to get back on the road, and Paige is now hiding in another hotel room. Wind Valley isn't the same as big cities. And as much as I wish she were here with me, I get it. Well, I get as much as I need to.

Still, I'd love to include her in this part of my life.

I love book signings, but knowing Paige is waiting for me makes me itch to rush out of here.

So I settle for sending her a quick "wish you were here" text, and then I get to work signing books and taking pictures.

I'm a grown man, but the clock is running low on my time with her. The fewer people I have to share her with, the better. Plus, on our way back to Wind Valley, I have a few stops in mind to help her cross more off her bucket list. The first stop is a hair salon my sister recommended where Paige can dye her hair purple. I'm not so sure she'll go through with it, but it's on the list.

A loud laugh at the table next to me pulls my attention.

Bailey Gold. She's on her fourth book and just got picked up by Vans and had a movie deal last year. Her line is longer than mine has ever been, and that says a lot because I've never not had one, but still. I want that. I want that next step. I'll say it over and over until it happens.

Paige could help me make it happen, but hell, how much did we complicate things over the two days?

Physically, we made them better, but for the sake of this deal, I could have just screwed everything up.

I sign another book and smile for another picture. Then the doors open, and a distinct whisper among the crowd begins. I pull my gaze from the current book in my hands to see Paige walking through the room. Although, walking might not be the word I want to use. She more like glides. She's wearing a T-shirt for one of my books and a long leopard print skirt, smiling and waving to strangers who point at her.

I growl, rising from my chair to meet her halfway.

She doesn't need me to defend her, but she also doesn't need people watching her like they are. If I can just get to her and keep her by my side, she'll be all right.

She smiles when she spots me, and the mere sight of her relaxes me.

A camera flashes.

I turn, ready to rip it from a fan's hands, reputation be damned. Paige stops me before I can do anything.

"It's okay."

"If that gets out, people will—"

"I know, but I want to support you. I can't do that from the room." She cups my cheek and crashes our lips together.

I hear the gasps and oohs and ahhs, but for once, I don't care that all eyes are on me. On us.

I know what I said I wanted in life, but that was before Paige walked into it.

Someone clears their throat next to me. I break the kiss.

Doug. My agent.

"Hi, yeah, hello, I'm Doug," he says and offers a hand to Paige. "I'm Graham's agent."

"Paige."

"It's a pleasure to meet you, but there are only about twenty minutes of this signing left, so if you two could keep that on pause till this is over, my fiancée would love it if I didn't miss my plane tonight."

"You're engaged?" I ask. "Since when?"

Doug gives me a look that screams *not now*.

Do the guys know about this? Doug is a part of our lives, but dang it, who knew he had a whole life of his own without us?

"Of course," Paige says. "I'll just walk around and browse."

"No way." I grab her hand. "The only place you're going is to my table with me."

Twenty minutes feels like two hours.

Since I have another day of signing tomorrow, I leave my table set up and say goodbye to Doug. Then, after about another half hour of waiting while Paige takes her picture with fans of her own, we're finally back in our room.

The door is barely shut before I pull her to me.

"What changed your mind?" I ask as she slips off her shoes.

"I told you. I want to support you. Plus, I sort of thought maybe people wouldn't care. The last couple of places, people didn't fuss. I hoped this would be the same."

I pull her to me and kiss the back of her shoulder. "Well, they loved you. I don't think I've ever seen fans so excited to take pictures with someone before."

"Oh god." She spins, her hands covering her mouth with a gasp. She lowers them slowly. "Do you think I made the other authors mad? Did I steal their spotlight?" Another gasp. "Are you mad? I should have asked you first. I can't believe I didn't ask you first. I just got your text, and I assumed."

This time, I kiss her forehead to soothe her. "It's fine. You didn't assume. I wanted you there. I didn't know it would end the way it did, but it doesn't change the fact that I wanted you there."

"Okay. Do you promise?"

"Yes."

"You'll tell me if that changes? I don't want to overstep, and you know I can't control what people post."

"I know you can't."

"Okay, but if—"

"Paige."

She takes a breath. "What?"

"Today was perfect."

With a hand on each side of her face, I seal her lips to mine. I'm not sure who melts more between the two of us. All I know is that this is exactly where I'm supposed to be, and this woman is exactly who I'm supposed to be with.

I spin her around, her hand clutching my shirt to hold on

as I bend just enough to hook my hands under her butt and set her on the hotel dresser. As soon as she's secure, her hand threads through my hair, and I groan.

The noise only fuels us to act with more desperation.

That's what it's like with Paige. I have no control. My body is starved for hers, and from what I can tell, the feeling is mutual. I can be a little rough at times, but her lack of commentary on the matter tells me she likes it.

"Take your shirt off."

She whips it off and then tugs at mine to untuck it from my jeans, pulling it over my head just as fast.

I step back, holding her hand so that she could stand.

With one more nod, I kneel to the ground and slowly slide her skirt and panties down her legs. Once she steps out of them, I hook a hand behind her right knee and lift her leg over my shoulder.

"This is officially my favorite thing to do to you. Since the moment I smelled you standing so close to me in the elevator. Since the moment I touched your silk-like skin on the couch in my hotel room. I knew you'd taste just as decadent as those moments. Having you near me has been torture, and I'm a lucky man that you trust me."

She inhales and moans when I give one long sweep of my tongue to her core.

"Graham."

"You're mine, Paige. Don't you forget it."

A slow smile touches her lips, and she nods. "Show me how you treat the things that belong to you."

Without missing a beat, I lift her leg higher and feast on her. Between my mouth and my fingers, I don't stop until she's riding my face harder than my fingers are driving into her.

"Oh god."

"Yes, baby. Let it out."

"Shit. Shit. I'm going to—ahhhhh!"

She cries out. The chances of the guests in the rooms around us hearing her are high, but I don't care. I want her to be loud. I want to be the reason she's loud and loses control. I want everyone to know that she's mine.

I slowly lower her leg to the floor and then carry her to the bed.

Her eyes are glazed, and her smile says that I did my job right. Obviously, the screaming and orgasm did that, too, but this look, the one she's giving me as I hover over her, is more than enough confirmation.

"I'm not done with you yet."

She sucks in a break. "I was hoping you would say that."

I reach between us and tug my jeans lower; my hard-as-rock cock springs free, and Paige grins.

I grip myself, rubbing my bare head against her, up and down, feeling her grow more wet with each swipe.

"I want to do this with nothing between us, but I need to know where you stand on that."

"I'm on birth control, and I'm clean," she says. "There hasn't been anyone in more than six months, and I was tested right before the wedding when I had suspicious thoughts of Vi—"

"Don't say his name, Paige, or I'll have to punish you."

She pulls her bottom lip into her mouth. "What other words earn me a punishment?"

"Fuck, Paige, don't tempt me. I'll come all over you

before I get to feel you, and that is not what I want right now."

Instead of replying, she reaches for me and guides me inside her.

"Oh, that feels good," she purrs. "Sooooo good."

I take my time, grinding my hips slowly and making it my purpose to get as deep inside her as I can before I circle my hips and then repeat the entire thing over again.

As soon as she starts to contract around me, I lose it. I grip her hips and pound into her, the sounds of her orgasm pulling every last drop out of me.

After I catch my breath, I dip into the bathroom, cleaning myself up and grabbing her a wet towel.

Once I crawl into bed, I pull her by the hip toward me. Not touching her is not an option.

Not when we have ten days left together at max.

Four weeks was not nearly enough time for us.

We can live in the bubble for now, but in just a matter of days, she'll be gone, and this part of our lives will close and that will be that.

Maybe I'll still see her from time to time. Maybe more if things work with me and her dad's company.

I'd ask if she's heard anything, but this isn't the right time. Hell, I'm not sure when is a good time at this point.

She nips at my lip and then swings her leg over my hips, snuggling into my side.

"I'm exhausted from this day. I'm ready to sleep."

I let out a light chuckle and then flip her over to her back.

"I don't think there will be much sleeping in here tonight."

She pulls her bottom lip into her mouth and smiles.

"I like the sounds of that."

CHAPTER TWENTY-TWO
PAIGE

My heart is racing, and I think I'm going to be sick.

I pace the hotel room and pat my hand against my leg.

As soon as Graham left for the morning signing, I knew it was time. The endless number of photos that appeared overnight with him and me in them paired with ludicrous headlines definitely mean today is the day.

Paige King dating again. Who is this mystery man? Paige King finds love in rehab! Paige King secretly cheating on Vincent Vellmont.

That last one makes me want to puke.

Still, I should have done this before last night. I should have done this days ago, but now I have no choice.

I should have rehearsed this. I should have written something out so I knew what to say. But I—

"Archie King."

Shit.

"Hi … Dad."

The line falls so dead silent, I hold the phone out far enough to see that we are, in fact, still connected.

"Dad?"

"Yeah, I'm here. Paige, is everything okay?"

I stop pacing and straighten.

"Yes."

"All right. Do you need something?"

"Um, just to call and check in and apologize for … a lot."

"Ah well, I'm at work. Can we schedule this later?"

"What?"

"Paige, I'm working, and your brother has kept me up to date. For some reason, you felt you could not come to me. I'm happy to hear you're doing well while off galavanting doing god knows what, but I have a business to run."

"Dad, I didn't think I couldn't come to you," I cut to it. Something I suppose I've already learned from Graham. "I just didn't want to hear the disappointment in your voice or see it on your face."

"You would be correct on that, but I'm not disappointed you left that man at the altar. I'm disappointed you felt you had to use your brother to update me. Now, I can pass you through to my assistant. We can arrange a lunch to discuss this further. Would you like that?"

"I'd like to not have to make an appointment with my dad."

"I see. I'll be in touch, Paige. It was good to hear from you."

With that, he hangs up.

What the hell was that?

I expected him to be mad or yell or even … I don't know.

But him telling me to make an appointment with his assistant was not what I was expecting.

"Shit." I sit down on the edge of the bed. This does not look good for me. It doesn't look good for Graham, either.

How am I going to swing this? I need to talk to Graham.

I glance at the clock. The signing should have ended at least two hours ago, which means he's probably in the hotel business center on his laptop by now. He told me he requested a late checkout so that he could get some writing in before we hit the road.

I grab my room key and take the elevator down to the business center.

Okay, I should prepare myself.

Graham, I know I said I'd get you a deal with my dad, but it turns out, I have no pull.

Ugh.

Graham, I talked to my dad, and it looks like I can't help you after all, but please don't let this affect what we have.

Gross.

Graham, I made this deal out of desperation, and now I can't hold up my end of the deal because I never called my dad after I ran out of my own wedding and ...

No matter what I say, I'm a mess and he deserves better.

I should just tell him the truth and book my ticket home. He's not going to want to look at me. Worse, he'll actually forgive me and thank me for being honest and then kiss me or something. Which would make me feel even worse, so I definitely can't go that route.

The business center is easy to spot. It's down a long hallway but the wall is all windows.

My steps slow as I spot Graham working.

This has to be said again: I cannot for the life of me get over how sexy this man is. How does he create scenes in his head? Do I inspire him? Has anything he's ever written actually happened to him?

"How's the book coming?" I ask before I stand here too long watching him.

"Good. It feels good to write."

He pulls me in front of him and then wraps his hand around me to grab my butt. In one move, his chair slides forward as he lifts me to sit on his lap.

I squeal.

"Someone can see us through all those glass doors."

"No one is coming down here." He peppers kisses along my neck.

"You don't know that. Someone else could be coming in here to get their daily word count in."

"Oooh, I love it when you speak my language."

"Graham Wright. We are in a public place, and now that people know where I am, maybe we should keep the touching and kissing to a minimum in public."

He sighs and rests his forehead against mine.

"You're right." He kisses me once more. "We should probably hit the road anyway. The sooner I get you back to my place, the sooner I don't have to hold back."

My heart beats faster.

"Um, well, before we go, there's actually something I want to talk to you about."

"If it's about all the photos online, don't worry about it. I've thought about it a lot today, and you know what? Everything goes in phases. In a couple of days, you and your new mystery man"—he winks at me— "will be old news. I know I hate having my face online, but this will blow over soon enough."

Well, it's nice to know where he stands.

"Actually, it's not about that."

He closes his laptop and shoves it into the bag, followed by a notebook and a few other random things.

"Well, in that case, hold that thought," he says with a grin. "I have a surprise for you."

Oh god, of course he does.

"Maybe I should tell you before the surprise."

He looks at me, his goofy smile slowly fading.

"Is everything okay?"

"Yes, and—"

A group of people step into the room.

"He should totally kiss her," one of them says.

"And more," another says.

Then they all stare at me and Graham for a split second.

"Act two should definitely start with a kiss," the third one says as she sets the computer in her arms down. "I agree."

Then they all sit down and open laptops, trading notebooks and pens between them.

"Come on," Graham says, his hand taking hold of mine. "Let's go to your surprise, and we can talk on the drive home."

I've lost my confidence to tell him at this point. It went right out the door as soon as he said *let's go home*. As if that's where we belong together.

The idea makes my mind spin with visions of a different future. Needless to say, we don't talk about Vans on the way home. But I do send my dad an email about Graham, and then I schedule an appointment to see him in a couple of weeks.

One way or another, I'm going to get Graham that contract.

This trip is supposed to help me find out who I am, and I want to be someone who keeps their word.

CHAPTER TWENTY-THREE
GRAHAM

Mornings are so much better with waking up to Paige in my bed.

Like right now, with the sun peeking through my curtains and shining on her purple-streaked hair.

Yep, that's right. She went through with it. She was so excited that, as soon as she was done, she snapped our first selfie so she could send it to Grace and her brother.

Both of them loved it, per Paige's words, and I guess her brother said he wanted to meet me.

It threw me off a little, because nowhere in this thing we have going on did she or I discuss meeting her family. I'm not sure why it would matter. Maybe for the sole purpose of knowing who was there for her after she made one of the biggest decisions of her life. Or maybe to see the guy who kept her from going back to marry the man waiting for her.

Ugh. That makes me sick but also a little nervous. What happens if I meet her family and then they say *oh, is this the guy who you want us to contract through Vans? No way, not after he's the reason you didn't come home.*

I mean, I'm not the reason, but I could be part of the reason now.

Maybe.

Shit. I don't know.

"If you rub your forehead any harder, you might start to lose some skin."

I grin at Paige's teasing words and drop my hand.

"Just needed something to do till you woke up."

I roll her onto her back and press a kiss to her lips.

"I have morning breath."

"I have morning wood. We both have issues. No biggie."

She burst out laughing. "How is it that no matter how much time we spend together, you can still shock me?"

"My mouth can do a lot of things that shock you."

She smacks my chest and then covers her face. "Stop. That was cheesy."

I'll be the cheesiest guy on the planet if it means I get this reaction from her. Her smile is my favorite thing in this entire world.

"What are we doing today?" she asks.

Up until today, if we haven't been doing something on her list, we've been crossing something off mine. I didn't realize how busy my life was until I added someone to it. I'm just lucky she has the time for me. For now anyway.

"The morning is pretty open, but in the afternoon, we're going to a barbeque at Tobias's house. He has a big one every year."

"It's Monday," she says as if that's a question and not a fact.

"Right," I nod. "Between the six of us, as you can see, schedules are hard to line up. Our first free day of the summer together fell on a Monday, so here we are."

"I love that you guys all still make time for each other. I can't remember the last time my friends invited me to something that wasn't for appearance."

I sit up higher on my bed, and she leans over me, her head resting on my chest.

"I'm not sure there's even one person, outside of Grace and Preston, that I'd call my best friend, and here you have five of them, plus spouses."

I rub my hand over her back.

"Yeah, I'm lucky. They remind me of that a lot."

She lets out a big sigh, and even though I have the urge to flip her over and take her right here and make this a new routine for how we start our mornings, something about lying with her here—naked, might I add?—and talking about something personal ... well, it feel more intimate than anything we've done so far.

"Hey, you know, if you want to do something random this morning, I'm your guy. Or if you want to do something spur of the moment, I bet one of the girls would go with you. You have a lot of options here. What do you want to do?"

She taps her chin and pretends to think good and hard.

"Let's go to a movie."

"A movie?"

She nods. "And get popcorn and candy and soda."

"You don't do that at home?"

"Not unless someone has cleared the theater at least two hours ahead of time and they can get me in the back door."

I stare at her.

I know her dad is number one on Forbes right now, but that lifestyle is just … a lot. She might love parts of it, but I'm starting to understand the parts she doesn't a lot more.

Money doesn't always mean freedom or happiness.

"A movie it is."

"But first"—she climbs into my lap— "good morning," she says coyly and then kisses me, right before she grabs me and places me between her legs.

It's easy to forget that she won't be here forever because I'll tell you what, I could get used to mornings like this.

I can honestly say I've never been to a movie before noon in my life until today.

Truth be told, I wish I had done it sooner. I will forever be a matinee moviegoer from this moment on. One, there's hardly anyone in the theater and two, it's all the older people, and they sit up close, leaving me and Paige the prime seating in the back in the middle. It was amazing.

So was watching Paige immerse herself into the entire movie experience of Wind Valley.

I'm pretty sure she thought I was lying when I said we had only two theaters that each show only three movies at a time.

As soon as we got home, she left to grab sandwiches at the sub shop down the road while I made quick work with my daily word count.

That was the plan anyway. Until I saw an email from Doug.

The subject line read *call me, we need to talk about your dating life.*

It rings once before he picks up.

"Graham, hey, what's up?"

"You tell me. I got your email."

"Right. I just want to check in and see how things are."

"You just wanted to check in?" I doubt that. "You never call me about my dating life."

He blows out his breath. "That's because it's not my business."

"No, it's not."

"But when you're dating the daughter of a company we're attempting to work with and now you're being pictured with her all over the internet, I just want to make sure you know what you're doing."

I don't. I really don't. Enjoying every moment she gives me till she leaves is all I have, but I don't tell him that.

"It's nothing to worry about."

"Are you sure?"

"I'm sure."

"I just don't want this to hurt your chances with Vans."

"It won't, Doug. I've got this thing with Paige handled. Being with her isn't going to hurt my chances with Vans. If anything, it'll help them."

I turn in my chair to see Paige setting the food down. She waves, so I wave back.

"I have to go. We'll talk later."

"Yeah, okay. Bye, Graham."

I hang up and meet her in the kitchen.

"My agent thinks our relationship is going to hurt my chances with Vans."

"Oh." She lets out a small laugh. "Sounds like an agent."

"Yeah, but he doesn't know about our deal. So hopefully that call gives him a little less stress."

"Right," she says as my phone rings again.

"Simon, what's up?"

I grab my sandwich and head out onto the patio.

I maneuver our chairs so that we can sit across from each other, but when I look up, I see Paige at the table. Her back is to me.

"Are you listening to me?" Simon asks.

"No, sorry. Let me call you back—or hey, I'll see you at the barbeque, okay?"

I hang up and go back inside, taking the seat by Paige.

"Are you okay?" I ask.

She nods.

I set my sandwich down, grab the legs of her chair, and yank her to me.

She laughs when she almost falls over.

"Now tell me the truth."

"I was just thinking of the deal and our time together."

"Oh."

Fuck. If that's the face she makes when she thinks about it, I'm not sure I want to know exactly what she's thinking. If she's hurting from it, I'll hurt. This thing between us ... that's just how that works.

"What are you thinking?"

She shrugs and takes a bite of her sandwich.

I watch her the entire time until she swallows.

"You are relentless, Graham Wright."

"Only when it comes to you."

She grabs her soda and points the straw at me. "That. I

was thinking about that. I just … I really like spending time with you."

God, she is fucking adorable.

I grab her hand and kiss the back of it.

"This is the best summer I've ever had," I tell her.

It's true. What I don't tell her is that I wish it wouldn't end. That I've known her for three weeks, but I want years. I want decades. I want whatever she will give me as long as it's more.

But I don't say that because she makes a joke about our sandwiches and laughs.

She does that a lot around me, and I'd be a fool to take that from her.

So, like always, I'll just have to be happy right here and right now.

I don't want to miss moments like this because I'm too scared of what my future looks like.

CHAPTER TWENTY-FOUR
PAIGE

Paige

The sun has always done the mind and body good. And heaven knows I need some sun right now.

"I'm so happy you're here," Calla says as she skips toward the patio where Graham and I are. "Now we can get started on some games."

"Games?" I look at Graham. He shakes his head and rubs a hand over his face to hide his smile. He's too damn cute for his own good. Don't even get me started on lunch today.

He gave me an opportunity to tell him everything, but I couldn't do it. Not after he talked to his agent. *Being with her isn't going to hurt my chances with Vans. If anything, it'll help them.*

His response is branded in my brain. He didn't say it to hurt me or like he's using me. But we have a deal. No matter what has come between us, it still stands. I still just don't know how to make it happen.

"It's sort of a tradition but considering that I have zero books for the guys to give a title to if they win, maybe we should sit this one out."

Of course the games are about books. That's his life, and here I am bargaining his future just so I can have some fun for a few weeks.

I'm the worst.

Just in case, I look at my phone and refresh my emails. My dad has to email me back eventually. It's not in him to let any email go unanswered. But today, it seems, won't be that day.

"I call dibs on Graham's points," Simon says as he wonders toward us.

"Since when is that a thing?" Hero asks. "Tobias, is this a thing?"

Tobias shrugs. His focus is across the lawn where Natalie, Nora, and Willa are sitting.

"It can be."

Simon narrows his eyes and then turns to Graham. "We can't ask him when he isn't focused."

"Tell me more about these games?" I ask, and Graham opens his mouth, but Beck walks up.

"Basically," Beck says and hands us each a seltzer, "loser has to let the winner choose a book title for their next book. So if Graham loses, the rest of us get to name his next book."

"So it's a solo thing, or are there teams?"

Beck glances around and then shrugs. "Teams this year, I guess. There are enough of us."

"All right." Tobias shouts, and everyone immediately focuses. "This year, we have all new games, outside of one. As tradition, we've all hopefully hidden books around the house and yard. The group who finds the most gets five points. Next, we have decided to—yes, Simon?"

"Who is we?"

"We is me and Tobias," Natalie speaks up.

She and Tobias share a look I definitely want to ask Graham about later. I flash him a look over my shoulder, and he shakes his head.

"As I was saying, we've decided to switch things up this year. Writing games are too easy now. We're all great writers—yes, I'm just going to say it: we are pretty cool—so things we used to compete on now come easy to us. So!" He claps his hands.

"Get on with it!" Hero heckles him, cupping his hand over his mouth even though he's standing close enough to not need to do it.

"We're going old school!" Tobias rushes out.

Natalie flips open a cooler and pulls out balloons, red cups, and a few scarves.

"Umm, how old school?" Willa laughs.

"Super," Natalie says quietly. "I sort of forgot my half of the planning while Griffin and I were—"

"Moving on," Tobias yells, and Natalie just shakes her head and shrugs. "Are we ready?"

Everyone agrees and quickly divides into teams. Just as quickly, a table is lined with red cups and a pitcher of water.

"And this is?" I ask, pointing to the cups.

"Flip cup," Tobias says and winks at Zane. "Zane's favorite game."

"Oh, fuck off. I won at least once in college."

"Barely," Graham chimes in. "I think I had to flip for you."

Zane shoves him, and they all start to bicker about the college years.

I won't dwell on it because it's pointless now, but I wonder what life would have been like had I been able to take a more normal approach. College just isn't the same when you have a bodyguard and a list of classes so long, even sleeping seems impossible. But that's the way I wanted it. The sooner I was finished with college, the sooner I could step into the role of an executive director with multiple foundations.

"How do I play this?" I whisper to Willa who nods.

"We can be on the end. Trust me. Once you watch a couple of them, you'll get it."

And boy, is she right? Ten minutes later, I flip the cup once and it sticks.

We follow up that game with quarters and then another where my face still hurts from laughing so much. Whoever came up with the idea of having two people blindfold each other and try to pop the balloon between them as a game has a pretty great sense of humor.

"All right, we're on to the last competition of the night," Tobias shouts after a solid couple of hours of competition. "It's another new one, so be ready."

"Fuck, Tobias, really?" Simon shouts.

"Yes, you grumpy ass. Deal with it. Plus, this one is on Graham. Take it up with him."

Just then, Hero walks out of the house with a black box with two—oh my god.

"You did not," I say and smack him. I twist to face him and look up. "With all these people?"

"Better your friends than a bar filled with strangers."

"Graham."

I all but stomp my foot.

"It'll be fun."

"Karaoke!" Tobias shouts. "Duets to be more specific. Also a request from Graham."

He slings an arm around my shoulder. "We're in this together, remember?"

* * *

Before I know it, we're in the car and headed back home.

"Do you think Tobias will really let you guys name his next book?"

"Oh yeah." Graham nods. "We've all done it. He can't take it back."

"Do you think he'll be mad at Natalie for forgetting to hide his books?"

Graham rubs his chin and then shakes his head. "That woman could delete his entire backlist, and he still wouldn't be mad at her."

"So, he's in love with her?" I ask and roll my window down.

"I think so, but he's yet to admit it himself."

"Do you think he ever will?"

"I hope so. I'm afraid he'll regret it for the rest of his life if he doesn't tell her how he feels before it's too late."

His words hit close to home, and knowing Graham, he intended the double meaning behind them. The rest of the drive is silent.

"Did you have fun?" he asks after he parks the car, and we get out. He reaches for my hand; I spin to him and wrap my arms around his neck.

"I did. I don't get to go to many laidback gatherings, so that was nice."

"Laidback gatherings," he repeats. "Is that the proper term for boring?"

"No." I lean in to kiss him. "It means I had a great time. I like your friends. I like Wind Valley. It's refreshing, and it's been exactly what I needed. The fact that not a single person here has tried to take my picture is comforting too."

His hand brushes the hair from my face as he towers over me and looks into my eyes. It's as if he's trying to tell me something without using words.

You. You're exactly what I needed. That's what I want to add, and hopefully, that's what he's trying to tell me, but I don't say anything, and he doesn't either.

Graham is an open person. I imagine if there was something he wanted to say, he'd say it. So it doesn't surprise me that my mind is running wild with what he could be thinking.

He presses his thumb to my forehead. "You'll get a wrinkle if you keep thinking that hard."

I roll my eyes and playfully push him back before I head up the steps.

"What's on the agenda for this weekend?" I ask, changing the subject to something lighter. I'd love to stand here and tell him every single thing on my mind, but that would mean telling him that another day has gone by, and my dad still hasn't replied to me. I even emailed him again during the BBQ. It might be overkill, but I can't not do anything.

I really don't want to let Graham down, but the more days that go by and the more I fall for him, I'm afraid that I have no control over the outcome.

As much as I'd love for this to end happily for us, for *him*, I'm not so sure I can make that happen.

CHAPTER TWENTY-FIVE
GRAHAM

It's Friday.

What might seem like a typical day to most people is the day I've been dreading.

Well, I was dreading it until I woke up this morning.

This weekend is, per our deal, the last weekend Paige is here. It's the last weekend we have together. Next week she's supposed to be gone, and I'm supposed to have a contract with Vans.

Has it crossed my mind that it's weird she hasn't once mentioned it? Yes. But we never really set terms on when she'll reach out to her dad, so it's possible she's waiting until my half of the deal is finished. Which is technically this weekend.

Hopefully, by Sunday night, all that will change.

Like I said before, waking up to Paige in my bed is something I could get used to. I want to get used to it, and there is only one way to make that happen. I've thought about it all week long.

Paige said she loves it here. My friends think she's amazing. My family likes her, and me— well, I think it's pretty clear how I feel about her.

So, I made a plan. It's been a long week of keeping this from her, but if I want to show her how she can have everything in her life and still be with me here in Wind Valley, I'm going to have to take a chance.

I planned a camping trip for the weekend, and I invited a couple of guests.

"Hey," Paige says, walking out of my room with her hair in a messy bun and wearing only one of my T-shirts. "How much do you have left?"

She nods to my computer where I'm just saving today's work.

"I'm actually done. Why?"

"I was thinking we could go to the waterfall here today or maybe go on a hike. Do something that you like to do instead of crossing something off my list. I don't have much left."

"We need to finish that list and add more to it."

"We will."

She rests her hip against the kitchen counter and plays with the hem of the shirt.

The vibe I'm getting is that she's also thinking about this weekend and what it means. I'd cave right now and ask her, but I have this whole plan in place for the weekend, and I think my chances of her saying yes are higher if I wait. I don't want her to say yes because she's afraid of what will happen if she leaves. I want her to say yes, that she'll stay here with me in Wind Valley, because she pictures her life here.

I stand from the table and stalk toward her.

She starts to smile, but I cup her chin and kiss her hard before she can do a damn thing.

Then I grab her hips and plop her on the counter, spreading her legs so that I can stand between them.

I glance at the clock on the stove.

Her surprise is going to be here any moment, but that doesn't mean we can't try to have a little fun first.

I slide a hand between her legs and curse. She's not wearing any underwear.

"Did you do this on purpose?" I ask and slide a finger inside her.

"Mmm, maybe."

I kiss her lips, her cheek, her neck, and then back up as my hand picks up the pace. She reaches for the waistband of my sweatpants, her hand reaching to pull me out. The heel of her left foot presses to my back as she scoots to the edge of the counter.

A knock at the door stops us.

I rest my forehead against hers and then kiss her as soon as I tug my pants back on. Meeting her brother with a hard-on isn't exactly in my plans, but I can't change that now.

"Hold that thought," I say when she reaches for me as I step back, rubbing my hands together. "I have a surprise for you."

A suspicious smile touches her lips.

"What is it?"

There is another knock at the door. "Do you want to put underwear on?"

She laughs and shakes her head.

"No, I think I'll let you go crazy knowing there isn't anything under here."

I practically growl.

"Go answer the door, then."

Her smile starts to widen as she hops off the counter to do just that.

"Did you have those big cookies delivered again?"

"Nope."

"Those crispy chicken salads from—"

"It's not food."

"Hmm." She taps her chin.

"Open the door already."

She lets out a giddy laugh and swings the door wide.

"Ahhh!" she screams and leaps into the arms of whomever is in front. I step closer. It's Grace. I don't see Preston.

Good thing, too, because my shirt has raised enough for me to get a peek of Paige's perfect ass cheeks.

I clear my throat, and Grace waves at me before pointing behind her. "His royal dumbass is getting the bags. We did the best two out of three with rock, paper, scissors, and he lost."

"My brother is here too!"

Grace grins. "I love that you know exactly who I'm talking about."

She enters the living room as Paige runs down the stairs.

I'm not even going to comment on the fact that she still isn't wearing panties and has now run outside where anyone could see her.

I'll just punish her later for it.

"Hi," Grace says and holds out her hand. "It's nice to officially meet the guy who has given our girl her spark back."

"Her? I think it's the other way around."

Grace shrugs. "Either way, I'm happy she's happy."

"Me too. Hopefully, she'll be happy when I tell her we're going camping for the weekend."

"She's going to love it. You did good."

A moment later, Preston and Paige are both coming through the door.

"I just can't believe you're here. This is so exciting. Graham is amazing, and I know you'll love him."

"I still can't believe you have purple hair," he says and laughs. "You've wanted purple hair since you were thirteen."

"I know," she says and claps. "Just wait till you hear all the things I've been doing."

"I'm glad you made it safely," I say and offer my hand. "Graham Wright."

"Preston King. It's nice to finally meet you. With all the pictures of you two, it feels like I've known you forever."

He has a point. The photos aren't overwhelming, but at least one new one of Paige and me from my last signing pops up every day. Nothing in Wind Valley though, and I'm grateful for that.

"It's nice to meet you too."

"Before we get this shindig on the road," her brother says, "how about you get dressed, sis?"

"Oh." Paige blushes. "Yes. That's a good idea."

She walks past me to get to our room, winking.

I'm tempted to follow her, but I think the lack of clothing might be enough for her brother right now.

She's back seconds later, still in my shirt but with a pair of shorts on too.

"So, what's the plan now? How long are you guys here?"

"All weekend," Grace says and sits on the couch.

Paige kisses my cheek and then wraps her arms around my waist.

"Thank you."

"Don't thank me yet—you still need to pack."

"Pack?"

I nod. "Yep, all of us are going camping."

Her laughter makes the entire room smile.

"Preston, camping?" she says and laughs harder.

"That's what I said," Grace chimes in.

"Oh, stop it. I can camp. I showed up, didn't I? And I knew about it before you."

"When do we leave?" Paige asks.

"As soon as you're ready" is all I get out before she dashes back to my room.

"Give me five minutes."

About twenty minutes after that, we're on our way down the steps with the last of our things to load into my truck. Paige is in front of me, bouncing down the steps with excitement.

Her phone dings just as we step into the parking lot, stopping her in her tracks and causing me to bump into her.

"Hey, whoa, is everything all right?"

Her gaze snaps up to me and she drops her phone into her purse.

"Great. Yes. Why do you ask?"

I study her for a moment. Her entire light and cheery vibe she'd had seconds ago is gone. "You're being weird."

"I'm not being weird." She lifts up to her toes and presses a kiss to my lips. I slide a hand around to her lower back, ready to deepen the kiss, but she pushes me away.

"My brother is on the other side of the car, Graham."

"So?" I pull her back to me. "You had no problem running to hug him in nothing but my shirt earlier."

"I was too excited to think straight."

She smiles, kisses my cheek, and then skips away.

I watch her, because hell, it's hard not to. If she's anywhere near me, my eyes are on her.

She stops at the back of the car, says something to Grace, and then pulls her phone back out.

All happiness drops from her features as they both look at the screen.

Whatever caused her to stop suddenly, it isn't good. And from the way she brushed it off with me too quickly just now, she clearly doesn't want to tell me about it.

I hate that.

It gnaws at my chest, but maybe once I ask her to stay here with me, she'll finally see how serious I am about her, and she'll share whatever this is with me.

"Hey," she shouts and opens the car door behind the driver's side. "Are you coming?"

"Yep." I shoot her wink.

Everything will change after this weekend, and I can't wait to spend more time with her. Thoughts of the night we met hit me as I get into the driver's seat. I wanted to step outside my box because I wasn't going to find someone to settle down with if I didn't, and it actually worked.

Find me *the* woman to spend forever with. Check.

CHAPTER TWENTY-SIX
PAIGE

I've never had to fight back tears so hard in my life.

I lean into the window and open the email from my dad again. I stare at the picture of Graham kissing me, with me on his lap in that damn business room at the hotel. Then I read the two words under it.

Sorry. Pass.

What am I supposed to tell Graham?

The deal was that if he took me with him, I'd help, but it turns out, being with me did the exact opposite.

Shit.

We head down another dirt road until we slowly creep up on a meadow that has three tree horseshoe areas to the right of it. It's almost as if someone intentionally planted trees in the shape of a U three times just to make this area.

"We can each put a tent under each set of trees." Graham smiles and points to my right. "And there's a river just over there for fishing."

Despite the way my heart hurts right now, I smile.

I should tell him, but he's been so focused on helping me do all these things, I can't bring myself to do it.

I had one job. One thing to offer, and I couldn't do it. Then, all because I wanted to show him how much he meant to me and step back into the spotlight, I cost him his dream.

My time with Graham isn't over yet. I can still turn this around.

I take a breath and start to type out a reply. I know I'm not part of the publishing company, but Graham is an amazing writer. Vans would be stupid not to take him on as an author.

My thumb hovers over the keyboard on the phone.

Please reconsider doesn't seem like it's good enough. The emails I've sent said everything I could think to say about Graham's books. Plus, whatever I reply with has to be perfect. Obviously, my dad thinks I'm asking him for this because Graham and I are more than friends. I need to word this carefully. Taking a little time to get it right is what I need to do. Hopefully, this fresh air will clear my mind and help me find the words.

"I can't believe we're really doing this," my brother says as Graham opens the tailgate of his SUV and starts pulling out the three coolers we brought.

"I can." I beam.

"All right, the part I'm talking about is how some people still use tents instead of buying a camper." He looks directly at Graham.

I roll my eyes and smile. "You'll be fine."

"Oh, I know I will. I just don't understand why people do it when they have better sleeping options for the woods."

"You're such a diva," Grace says and takes a sip of her water. "Maybe you should go back."

The glare my brother gives her makes me want to laugh, but I don't, of course.

"So I think we could set up one tent right there." Graham points out a spot where the ground is flat. "And there. That would leave the center horseshoe for a firepit."

"And the third tent?" my brother asks.

"I only had two, but—"

"You only had two?" my brother asks with zero emotion in his voice. "And the store didn't have one more you could buy? Any store."

"Oh, I'm sure they did, and I—"

"No worries. I brought my own," Grace adds. "I like to be prepared."

My brother lets out a noise I'm unfamiliar with and then crosses his arms. "I hate to admit this, but that was smart thinking, Grace."

"Oh hell." She moves past us to start setting up her tent. "I told Graham I had a tent. That's why he only brought two."

Preston rolls his eyes and walks away.

Before we know it, everyone's sleeping arrangements are set up and there's a fire going as the sun begins to set behind us.

"We should have come out here sooner," I say as I sit in my chair. It's a rocker, and I absolutely love it. I had no idea they made camping chairs this fancy.

Despite my worries over what to say to my dad, this air and quiet and being right here relaxes me. Just as I needed.

"We'll have plenty more weekends," Grahams says, reaching over to squeeze my hand.

My gaze meets my brother's across the fire.

I know what he's asking without actually using the words, and the truth is, I don't know the answer.

This thing between Graham and I goes way past the time I have left, but what happens if that changes because I can't get him this deal? Deep down, I don't think he would do that, but another part of me doesn't want to lose this happiness I wasn't so sure I'd ever find.

Everything feels so complicated. I know what I want, but I don't want to make the wrong move and lose it.

"I'm beat," Grace says, standing to stretch. "I'm going to bed early."

Preston stands too. "I'm not tired, but I'm tired of sitting next to this fish bait shit."

After our campsite was set up, we went fishing. We were there for three hours, and one fish was all I had to show even though I let him go. I'm damn proud of myself.

"Good night," I say and wave as they both head for their tents.

Graham stands quickly, grabs my hand. Once we're inside our tent, sitting on our bed, Graham slides his hand around my back and jerks me toward him.

"What are you doing?"

"What do you think I'm doing? I'm finishing what we started in the kitchen this morning."

"My brother could hear us," I say, biting my bottom lip to keep from making any kind of noise. Graham kisses my neck and moves lower.

I will never, ever, grow bored with the way his mouth

feels on my body. Just one touch from him and I'm a goner. I hope this feeling never goes away.

"Then I suggest you be very, *very*, quiet."

He kisses me hard then, his hand sneaking into the front of my sweats.

"I'm not so sure that's possible with you," I manage to say and strip down before getting under the covers. We debated sleeping on bare dirt but agreed that an air mattress was just as good.

Graham's soft chuckle makes me clench my knees together as he crawls over me.

"I'm going to take what you just said as a compliment," he says and pushes them apart.

He starts slowly, taking his time as he strokes his tongue over me.

I try to buck my hips at the sensation that it brings me, but his arm clamps down over me, holding me in place.

"Don't move."

"I have to," I say.

"Why?"

"If I can't cry out from the intensity, you have to let me move."

"Just grab my hair if you want to scream and keep your hips down." His words are hushed, and then he's spreading my legs wider as he feasts.

It doesn't take long for my body to build up the tension he created, so I grab his hair.

I tug so hard that he growls and picks up the pace.

Fuck. Fuck. Fuck.

That's all I can think of. I can't say a word, so I pull hard, and his tongue moves faster.

And faster.

And faster.

"Shit!" I yell and then slap my hand over my mouth.

Graham acts as if he didn't hear a word, never letting up until my release successfully takes over.

I close my eyes, but I know without a doubt that my vision would have gone black even if they were open. The orgasms I have with Graham are out of this world. I swear, if it weren't for the pounding of my heart, my body would feel like it's floating when he does this to me.

I'm barely regaining my composure when he yanks his shorts off and flips us so that I'm on top. His hand strokes me, and I buck, clearly sensitive to the touch from what he just did.

"Can you take any more?" he whispers.

I nod, and then grab him, stroking to match his pace.

His head drops back when I guide him between my legs and lower over him.

"Fuck," he says loudly. Just like I did to myself, I slap my hand over his mouth.

He grabs my wrist, ready to move it, but I shake my head and lean forward until my lips are next to his ear, my hips still grinding over him.

"If you want me on top, I call the shots."

His eyes light up.

I pull my hand back and start to circle my hips when he says, "Don't go home next week."

My heart pounds. "What?"

"Don't go. Stay with me in Wind Valley."

"For … for how long?"

"As long as you want. Paige, I don't want this to end yet."

I lean down to kiss him, my hips moving a little faster now.

"Neither do I. Okay, I'll stay."

I'll remember his smile at this moment for the rest of my life.

I'm not going to ruin the weekend by telling him about my dad's email, but as soon as we're home, I have to tell him. Because let's face it, if I want to be with him, there's no way around it now.

CHAPTER TWENTY-SEVEN
GRAHAM

Walking into my condo on Sunday night feels a whole lot different.

This time, there isn't some ticking timeline of never seeing Paige again, and it feels pretty fucking good.

As soon as we got home, Paige, her brother, and Grace went to grab sandwiches while I got in my word count. They won't be gone long, so I'll get a thousand words at most, but I'll take it.

I'm just finishing up when my computer freezes.

"No, no, don't do that. Don't do that."

I wiggle the mouse, but the cursor doesn't move.

Fuck.

I blow out a breath and focus on the fact that I'd saved my draft before we left, so the only words I'll lose are tonight's. Tomorrow I'm going to get a new computer. I can't take chances like this.

I force shut it down and pray that everything will come back up as soon as I turn it back on.

I can hear noise outside the door. Paige. My shoulders relax.

My computer restarts as soon as they walk in the door.

I breathe out a sigh of relief as the screen pops up, but then suddenly, every app on my computer starts to flash open.

What the heck? Jesus, when computers decide to give up, they sure do go all-out, don't they?

"Everything okay?" Paige asks.

"Yeah, just a computer on the fritz, but nothing I can't fix tomorrow."

I'm about to get up and help her in the kitchen when the flashing apps stop and the last one catches my attention.

It's from Vans Publishing. Archie Vans, to be more specific.

Holy shit.

Holy shit!

It's happening, it's—wait, the subject line has a re: in it, meaning he's replying to my email ... only, I never emailed him.

I scan the body of the message quickly, taking in the photo of me and Paige and the simple two-word reply under it.

Sorry. Pass.

What is this?

So I look back at the email before it. It's from Paige to her dad.

Suddenly, I'm glancing from dates to times and scrolling quickly to see all the emails in the chain.

Her dad passed on signing me two days ago, and she didn't reply.

I look over the emails again, trying to piece it together. Okay, so she sent her first email to him a couple weeks ago, which isn't when we made the deal, but okay, that's fine, she still reached out to him per our deal.

I go back to the most recent email.

He passed.

Fuck.

I stare at the photo and shake my head.

Is this why he passed?

I really am going to be stuck in this spot. Maintaining. Being a mediocre writer who has good books but not books great enough for the big screen or billboards or awards.

Hell, that hurts.

But you know what stings even more? Paige never replied.

My hand rests over my heart.

Even she doesn't think my books are worth fighting for.

She just … accepted it and went on with her life. And it's been two days. Was she ever going to tell me? And why does the wording of her first email make me think she didn't really care to try? That she never believed in me.

"Well, when you get home, I can tell you for certain that the foundation is going to be happy to see you. Your partner has been galivanting all over LA, and it's not looking good. You have a lot to save for the reputation."

I slowly turn to look into the kitchen, where Paige is standing across from her brother.

He's talking to her as if she's going home, but I asked her to stay, and she said yes. But now, shit, has anything she's told me been true? Is she just saying things to make me happy until she has what she wants?

Time away from her life that she clearly plans to go back to.

Paige doesn't answer her brother, but her gaze snaps to mine. I don't have time to decipher the look she gives me because it quickly turns to concern.

"What's wrong?" she asks and moves toward me.

I stand and back up, which causes her to stop.

"I …" I start and point at my computer. "All your accounts are still linked to my computer from when you were using my iPad."

"Okay …"

"And I saw the emails with your dad." I make a weird huff of frustration. "Or the lack thereof?"

Instead of replying, she looks at Grace.

What the fuck does that mean?

"Preston, let's give them a moment," her friend says, tugging on his arm. Her brother glances between us before he follows her out the front door.

Oh fuck. If Grace knows what's up, this can't be good.

Every scenario of what Paige might say runs through my mind, but I've landed on "she used me to escape her life." She never planned to help me get in with her dad, and she never planned to stay here. She was always going to go back, and that's why she never told me. Once she was gone, what would it matter, right?

As soon as we're alone, she finally speaks up. "I was going to tell you."

Since I've already built up her side of the story, I laugh. It's a good hearty laugh too.

"Right, yeah. Right after you got home and got back to work with your foundation, I'm sure."

"Don't do that."

"Do what, Paige? You lied to me."

"I didn't think that—"

"That you'd have to tell me the truth. Yeah, I get that."

Her hands go to her hips, and she glares at me.

"Let me talk. You can't argue with me if you don't know my side."

"Your side is pretty fucking clear."

"No, you do not get to do that. You do not get to judge me. If anyone knows me, the real me, it's you, and I will not accept that this one mistake is going to ruin everything we—"

"Everything we had was a joke to you."

She inhales and shakes her head as a tear runs down her cheek.

"Please stop interrupting me. I just want to explain."

"Explain what?" I snap, and she flinches.

Fuck, now I feel guilty for snapping.

"Ahh," I growl and grab the back of my neck. "Your first email to your dad explains it all."

I pull it up so I can read it to her.

"Dad, I wish our phone call had been longer the other day, and I can't wait for lunch when I get back." I stop and look at her. "When you get back," I repeat. "Until then, please check out romance author Graham Wright. He's been self-publishing since the start, and his books are really great. I know I'm not a part of the Vans team, but maybe you could look into him for me anyway. Love, Paige."

She doesn't say anything. She just stands there with her arms folded in front of her as she cries quietly.

"Maybe you could look into him for me *anyway*," I say one more time. "You really sold me there, didn't you? And then he passed, and you said nothing."

I shake my head.

"Every morning that you were here, I woke up and thought, *how can I make today perfect for her? How can I help her cross something off her list? How can I show her how much she means to me? How can I—*" I rub my hands over my face. "How can I convince her to stay? All the while, you sent three whole emails hoping he'd *maybe* look into me, and then just accepted a no."

I swallow and clear the lump that's formed in my throat.

"Graham, I ..."

"I think you should go with your brother when he leaves tonight."

I stand slowly, grabbing my sandwich, because even though my heart feels like it's under a junkyard compactor, I will not starve, and head for my room.

"No, I want to stay here and fix this. I want to stay here with you."

I pause and look at her over my shoulder.

"And after all this, how can I believe anything you say to me?"

She breaks into a full-on cry, and as much as I want to hold her and kiss her and tell her that I'm sorry I made her cry, I won't.

Every day that I spent with Paige, I thought that perhaps my career isn't where I needed to make a change. Maybe meeting her and bringing her into my world and getting to know hers was exactly what I was looking for. I didn't need to advance my career as long as I had her.

Hell, was I wrong or what?

For a man who just couldn't wait to fall in love, it fucking sucks.

CHAPTER TWENTY-EIGHT
PAIGE

This place doesn't feel like home anymore.

I mean, I know I'm not at home right now. I'm at the office where I've always come to do work on the various foundations I manage, but honestly, I could answer emails from anywhere.

I lean back and spin my chair to look out the windows behind my desk. When we had the building designed, I asked for these windows so that I could look out over the city anytime I was here. Vincent had told me that we wouldn't need to work from the office, but I'd thought differently. This foundation is important to me, and when I love something, I want to be there for it. Now, I sort of think maybe it was an excuse to have a space of my own. To escape the life I'd built with him.

I do love what we stand for here, but as I look out at the city, I wish I were looking at a mountain backdrop. At random neighbors who still read a newspaper and drink their coffee on their patio. I wish I could hear the sound of coffee being made behind me as I, too, sit on our patio. And then I'd hear Graham's chair sliding against the kitchen floor as he sits at the table to write. I wish all I had to do was stand and walk through one set of doors until I found him. Until I kissed him. Until he kissed me back.

But I don't have that. All because I just didn't tell him the truth.

It would have been a five-minute conversation that ended a whole lot differently than the one we had last night. Sure, we might have fought. But it would have been a different kind of fight. Maybe we could have found a solution together.

I turn back around to my computer and look at the never-ending list of emails. I'd planned to be out of the office the past month anyway—you know, back when I was supposed to be on my honeymoon. God, that feels like a completely different life now.

As if that life knew I was thinking of it, Vincent appears in my doorway.

"Wow. You're here."

I stare at him. I have no words. I should probably comment on how he never once texted or called me after I walked out on him, but I don't have it in me. If I'm going to fight to fix a relationship, it's not going to be with him.

"No hard feelings, right?" He goes on after I still don't say anything. "I mean, you're back now. All is well. How was your trip, by the way? You could have totally done your job from there, but Wyoming?" He laughs. "We're big city people. Anything smaller than LA is not who you are, so you made the right choice. I'll have my assistant email you a schedule for the next month. You might want to fix your hair and get a facial. Your skin is looking a little dull, and then here is the …"

You know that moment in books and movies where the smallest thing someone says or does makes everything click for one of the main characters? Vincent's words fade out because, yeah, it just happened to me.

This life, here, is not where I'm supposed to be. Like he said, I can run this foundation from anywhere, and it's damn time I did too.

Life with Graham in Wind Valley was so much more relaxing. He cared about me, not all those things Vincent listed. The things my old life was filled with.

I miss Graham. Who cares if it's only been one day?' That's one day too many. I miss him so much it hurts to think about what I'm supposed to do next without him. Which is exactly why I slap my computer closed, stuff it in my bag, and walk right out of my office without a single word to Vincent.

I don't even turn around as he yells my name.

I just get on the elevator, take a car to the Vans building, and walk right past my dad's assistant.

I am so sick of not doing what I want or being too scared to fight for it.

"Did you even read my emails?" I ask, marching into his office and closing the door behind me. "Or if you did, did you even look into Graham's history as a writer?"

"It's great to see you too, Paige. How are things since you've been home?"

I know the tone. It's his 'let's try again' tone. I grew up with that tone and heard it more times than I needed to. Before, I'd do exactly as he asked, but not today.

"My emails about Graham Wright. Did you read them?"

He sighs, leans back in his chair, and folds his hands in front of him.

"You want me to sign a contract for the man who whisked you from a wedding you ran out on? I didn't hear from you for almost two weeks. I only knew you were okay because you called your brother. When you did call, you just said sorry but provided no explanation. Then suddenly, you and this guy I've never met are all over the internet and you email me for a favor. Do you see where I'm going with this?"

"I do, and I get it. You're right. I should have done so many things differently, but I didn't. But Dad, Graham's books are amazing. You've been trying to get more movies with Netflix and Hulu, and I think this would be perfect. His back-list has twenty-plus books, the reviews are incredible, and he's still writing. His following is insane. He's always open to new ideas, and he—"

My father holds his hand up, and I stop talking.

"This is not how this works, Paige. If he wants to be a part of this company, he or his agent need to reach out."

"They have, and he hasn't heard anything."

"Then they should take that as a pass. It's only business."

He nods as if the conversation is done and rolls his chair forward to get back to work.

"No." I sit in the chair across from him. "People use connections all the time in business, and I'm Graham's connection. Not because of my relationship with him, but because of who he is as a writer. I'm not leaving until you find out who received the email from his agent and made the choice not to sign him."

"Paige."

The warning tone is there again, but I don't care anymore. I made a deal with Graham, and I'll be damned if the last thought he has of me is that I couldn't hold up my end of the bargain or that he couldn't trust me to do what I said I'd do. Sure, at first, I didn't care if I could, but things are different now. I'm different now. I don't want to be someone who stands back and waits to be told what to do, who sits around thinking she doesn't like her life. I want to make my own choices and get shit done. And right now, my choice is to find out why Graham's books aren't good enough for Vans and change their minds.

"I'm not leaving until you get me an answer."

"Then you'll be waiting here a long time."

"Okay," I say with a nod. "Do you want to hear about what I did while I was gone?"

"I have work to do, Paige."

I bite my lip, and for a moment, I consider that what I'm doing could be perceived as childish, but not in my eyes. In my eyes, I'm relentless, straight from Graham Wright's playbook, and that's what matters. I won't go down without a fight.

"I learned how to roller skate."

Nothing.

"I learned how to fish."

Nothing.

"I took Preston camping."

This one actually causes him to stop typing, but he doesn't look up or say anything. I guess I need to bring out the big guns.

"I went skinny-dipping in a pool, and it was—"

He jams a button on his desk phone. "Amy, call Calvin up here."

"Calvin? Is that your security?" I ask with a laugh.

The expression on his face is so serious, I'm probably right.

Shit. What's my Plan B?

"Dad. Don't toss me out, okay? Please consider Graham's books. He's a great writer. He knows love, and he will bring in an audience that could change the company."

"Paige—"

"If it's reputation, then you should know that he's kind, and he's sweet. He's considerate, and he puts everyone else first, and he helped me when I was scared. I didn't want to marry Vincent, and yes, Graham was a stranger, but he helped me, and he took care of me, and he worried about me, and he—"

"Paige!"

Whatever he was going to say next is interrupted by Amy walking in with a man in dress pants and button-down shirt.

That doesn't look like security.

"Sir, you asked for me?" Calvin says.

My dad nods. "Graham Wright. Have you heard of him?"

Calvin nods. "Yes, sir."

"Tell me what you know. In less than five sentences."

"He's a bestselling indie author who has topped the charts in the top five with every release in the past couple of years. He's based out of Wyoming and is represented by Doug Sharpe. He's won multiple indie awards along with nominations for best author with *Lovers Magazine* for the last five years. At least three of his books can be found in the top one hundred at any given time."

My dad makes an *umph* noise and looks at me.

"Search for a submission request from Doug Sharpe. Let's take a closer look at Mr. Wright to see if he could be a potential author for us. Don't send a contract until you speak with me again."

"Yes, sir."

Calvin leaves without another word, and I cannot control the smile on my face.

"Thank you."

"Well, it seems Mr. Wright might have done this on his own. Perhaps you should be his agent. I've never seen you this persistent."

"It's fun," I say, then stand. "Does this mean you never actually read my emails?"

"It means that my daughter had just run away from her entire life, and I didn't trust her judgment."

"Understandable."

I turn to leave.

"Did you find what you were looking for over the last month?" my dad asks.

Memories of sitting on the patio drinking coffee, eating sandwiches in a field, screaming on a roller coaster, singing karaoke, riding in a car, running and jumping on a Slip N Slide, and so much more flash through my mind. All of them include one face smiling back at me, and every single one of them makes me feel one thing: like I finally belong somewhere.

"Yeah, I did."

"And what will you do now that you have it?"

That's the thing, isn't it? I don't have it, not anymore. No matter what outcome comes from Calvin looking into

Graham, he told me to go. He wanted me to leave. End of story.

I shrug, and Dad laughs.

"After all that," he gestures to where I'd been sitting, "you do great work, Paige, but I've never seen you so passionate or determined not to fail. So, your answer is really that you don't know."

"Well, I know what I want, but even though I planned to go back to Wind Valley after I talked to you, I'm not sure what the outcome will be. Graham was really mad at me when I left."

He folds his hands in front of him and he's about to say something when my mother walks into his office.

"Paige," she says quietly as her gaze falls on me. For a split moment, I think she's going to yell or scold me or anything really for running out the way I did, but she doesn't. Instead, she rushes to me and hugs me in my seat.

"I love you, dear, and I'm so happy to see you."

I hug her back.

"I love you too, Mom."

My father clears his throat.

"I hate to cut this short for you two, but Paige, you just spent four weeks with this man. If you love him the way I can see that you do, you know what you need to do. Take some of the Paige you just brought in here with you. She's going places."

"Thanks, Dad," I say and then walk around his desk to hug him too.

"Now git."

"And call your father and I when you get there this time," my mother adds.

I laugh. "You got it!"

I rush home, schedule a flight for first thing in the morning, and start packing my bags.

I plan to be gone much, *much* longer than four weeks this time.

CHAPTER TWENTY-NINE
GRAHAM

I'd been so caught up with Paige this last month that I almost missed the opening of Simon and Tobias's new business.

It's a shared working space in the heart of Wind Valley. It's also right across the street from Willa's nutrition studio and around the corner from Beck's sister's coffee shop/library. Around the other corner is The Black Alcove bar. The location is prime real estate, and I couldn't be prouder.

Sales have been higher than normal since the first photo of Paige and I appeared. It's nice. Not exactly how I wanted people to find me, but they're new readers nonetheless, and I'm happy to have them. Still, each morning when I see the numbers, I think of Paige and feel … lost.

So being here right now, with friends, I need it.

"This place is great," I say to Tobias as he finally grabs a break from greeting guests and takes a drink of his water.

"Thanks." He rubs his neck.

"Is everything okay?"

"Huh? Oh, yeah."

His hand drops, and I can tell that the answer he gave me isn't the real one.

"Are you sure? We've known each other for a while. I think I can tell when something is bugging you."

He looks up as if he's debating on whether or not he should tell me what's on his mind.

"Um." He blows out his breath. "I remember when we started talking about starting a place like this back in college. Natalie used …" His words trail off, and he shakes his head. "It doesn't matter." Then he puts his arms out and grins. "We fucking did it."

Even though I know he's holding back, I grin, too, and chuckle a little. "Yeah, you did. Who knew we'd all be crushing our dreams ten years later?"

Well, most of us.

Paige left two days ago, and even after everything, I miss her. That makes me even more mad. Or sad—fuck, I don't know. Maybe I should have listened to her. She had a lot going on in the days leading up to our deal. I can't blame her for finally wanting something for herself. Still, I wish she had tried harder for me. Not because I needed that deal, but because she felt for me the way I did her. She didn't even fight for me. That's what gets me the most.

Screw the deal with Vans. They don't want me, fine. They don't want to be in my corner, supporting me and encouraging me to go on, fine. But Paige … she clearly wasn't in the same place as me: together. A team.

And then she left. I know I told her to, but maybe I wanted her to prove me wrong. I don't know. I should have done a lot of things differently, but at the end of the day, we're too different. It probably wouldn't have worked anyway.

"How are you doing, by the way?" Tobias asks. "Did you try to call her?"

I shake my head.

I told the guys everything on writing night yesterday, and they advised me to call her and actually talk to her instead of fighting.

It's a valid suggestion, but of course I didn't do it.

"No, but it's for the best. Despite what happened, we live different lives. She has cam—"

"Cameras in her face day in and day out and you want to remain out of the spotlight. I know. You've told us a million times."

"Then why do you ask?"

"Because, one, pictures of you did get out there, and aside from the whole publisher thing, your career is still thriving just as well as it was before. Two, at some point, you're going to realize that you aren't really mad over what happened, or that Vans didn't sign you. You're disappointed about how it ended with Paige, but instead of accepting that you still have time to fix it, you keep trying to convince yourself her social status is why you can't be together. So I ask because I want to know if you're going to let her get away or man up and go get your girl?"

He's right about all of it. I know he is, but the words don't register the way they should.

"I could ask you the same fucking thing."

"Whoa, whoa, what's happening out here?" Simon walks out of the back room. He crosses his arms and glares at both of us.

"Nothing." I shake my head at the same time Tobias says, "Just having a disagreement."

"About what?"

"Women."

"Ah," Simon says with a nod. He opens his mouth to say more but closes it.

"What?" I ask.

"It's nothing."

"Say it," Tobias says.

"Why? So I can be in a dick mood like the two of you?"

I let out a breath. "It doesn't matter what I think or how I feel. Paige and I didn't work out. It's over now. That's the end of the story." I shake my head as if all thoughts of her can be erased like an Etch a Sketch.

"This place really did turn out great, you guys. Sorry I'm in a shit mood."

"Thanks. I honestly didn't think this many people would show up. It's not like I offer food and drinks," Simon says. "Just workspace with Wi-Fi and free from the distractions of your house."

"Spoken like a true man who can't get anything done because he's worried about housework."

Simon shoves me. "I'm running a solo show. I need a break every now then for a few hours while Gray's at school. It's not a crime."

"I didn't say it was."

"Oh, Natalie is here. I'll be back," Tobias says and walks off.

"Do you want to talk about it?" Simon asks. "About Paige."

I shake my head.

My mind hasn't changed since Tobias just asked, but still, I know he means well.

Does it suck? Yes. Does a part of me wish she'd just walk through that door, proving me wrong on all my assumptions and fight for us? That she knows she should have talked to me and been open with me but was scared she would lose me because she loves me the way I love her?

Of course.

Hero, Beck, and Zane join us as if they were listening.

"Run it by us one more time," Beck says. "Just in case we missed something. Maybe we can come up with something else to help."

"Not going to happen. We didn't miss anything."

"Okay, well, if you won't talk about it with us, will you talk about it with her?"

Simon points over his shoulder.

My breath catches.

Standing right there in the doorway is Paige.

I set my drink down and approach her.

I don't want the guys to overhear this, but knowing them, they'll find a way.

"Hi," she says.

"Hi."

"I need your help."

She can't be serious. After everything she did, after she … hell, who am I kidding? My heart is hers, so if she needs me, I'm there. Even if she's going to leave me behind in the end.

"With what?" I ask and cross my arms.

She pulls out the notebook I gave her at the start of our summer road trip and shows me the list. Everything is crossed out but one line and that line has been circled with a Sharpie.

"I'm just going to cut to it since that's what I do now it seems. Meeting you the night before my wedding was the best thing that ever happened to me. I didn't know it then, but I think … I think that night I'd crossed off something I didn't even know should be on my list. That's why I jumped in your car. That's why I wanted you to let me join you all summer. That's why I made a deal with a promise I wasn't sure I could keep. All those choices meant I got to stay with you. I got to be happy and free and exactly who I wanted to be. As long as I was with you, I felt like I was home."

I swallow the lump in my throat and grab the notebook from her.

The line originally read "spend more time with Graham in Wind Valley," but now it reads "spend all my time with Graham in Wind Valley."

There are so many things we need to discuss, but first we need to clear the air.

"I messed up," she goes on. "I'm sorry. I shouldn't have made that deal knowing what I knew, and I should have come to you as soon as I knew I wasn't going to be able to make it happen. I still have one more thing on my list, and I totally get it if you tell me to leave again. I do. But I couldn't spend another day not telling you how sorry I am and that even if you don't want me in your life, I—"

"That's the thing," I cut her off and start to pace. "As messed up as this whole thing is, as mad as I am that you didn't talk to me, I can't stop thinking about you. I can't stop being in love with you."

There. I said it. Yeah, she messed up, but I know her well enough to know she didn't do it intentionally. Mistakes are going to happen in life. That's okay, as long as she does life with me.

"I can't stop wishing we had a future together, Paige. I just want you."

Her tears start to fall. It's a bubbly cry with a smile, but still.

I rush to her and brush them away, cupping her cheeks as she closes her eyes and takes a breath.

"And I sure as hell don't want to be the man who makes you cry."

"You can make me cry happy tears anytime you want."

"I'm so sorry that I blew up and didn't let you explain." I kiss her forehead.

"I'm sorry that I didn't talk to you when I should have. I just didn't want to lose you."

My heart swells. I step back and hold up the notebook.

"You wrote it down?"

"Well, yeah. If it's not on the list, it's not a guarantee to happen, right?"

"Right."

"Oh, I have one to add." She takes the notebook from me and scribbles something out.

She sets it on one of the tables and turns it to me.

Help Graham get a book deal with Vans.

"Talking to my dad didn't go as planned yet, but I visited his office before I came back here, and I'm not giving up. If you want it, I want it. That's how this works."

I pull her to me, cupping her face to kiss her again when someone knocks on the table next to us.

Tobias clears his throat. "Oh, hey, hi, I wasn't sure if you remembered me and this room that's full of people."

"Oh, we did," Paige snaps back with a smile. "We just don't care."

She pulls me in for a kiss, and I don't stop her.

I keep kissing her even after someone calls my name. I wrap my arms around her and grab her ass as her phone rings, but I still don't stop. The kisses don't even stop when she moans at my hand gripping the back of her shirt.

But then her phone starts to ring again, and we finally pull apart.

I groan. "Answer it."

She pulls it from her purse, and the name Calvin Redding appears.

"Oh!" she says quickly. "This is the editor my dad asked to look into you. Hello?" she answers quickly, never taking her eyes off me. "You did. When? Seriously! Thank you. Thank you!"

She hangs up and kisses me.

"Good news, we hope?" Tobias clears his throat. "Maybe G-rated too."

"Very." Paige starts to bounce in her spot. "Vans is offering you a contract. Doug should be calling you any moment."

"You're kidding!" I say so loudly that she startles, but then she laughs.

"I'm serious. A contract and the woman of your dreams telling you that she loves you all in one day." She fans herself. "If I didn't know any better, I'd say I went above and beyond my end of the deal, which is more than—Oh! Put me down!" She giggles against me as I toss her over my shoulder and march her right out the door.

"You can't be mad—you love me, remember?"

She laughs. "Yes, I love you."

"Good, because I love you too."

She's right, I got the girl and the contract all in one day.

It's time to go home and celebrate.

Naked, preferably.

EPILOGUE

SIMON

Another book finished.

I smile as I lean back and stare at the final sentence. Of course, I still need to write the epilogue and bonus epilogue, but I do those once the edits are finished.

I let out a light chuckle.

I never thought I'd finish this book.

Life has been so crazy lately that finding the time to write has been absolutely impossible. I'm over the 2:00 a.m. bedtimes, only to be awake by six to be sure my kid gets to school on time. I swear, he hit ten, and it's like he knows everything. It's his schedule or no schedule.

I have a hard time telling him no. I think that's the single dad in me who wants to make sure he gets everything he wants in life. I need to find a balance.

"Why are you grinning like that?" Tobias asks from across the table.

Tonight's writing night is just the two of us, so we're

writing out on my front porch. It's my favorite place to write. The table out here isn't big enough for more than two people. I've played with the idea of buying a bigger one, but the back of the house has a giant patio table, and this spot is turning into my sacred writing spot. I've finished two books in four months out here. If I were superstitious, I wouldn't change a thing.

Tonight's writing session was also a spur-of-the-moment deal. Tobias needed help with a plot issue, and my schedule, despite having a kid, is a bit more relaxed than the others in our writing group. The guys are all starting to settle down, and I couldn't be happier for them. It also means their schedules are busier these days.

"I finally finished this book," I tell him.

He claps. "There is no feeling like it. It's … happiness to see a story come full circle and dread that it also means you have to start the entire process over again for the next one."

I chuckle. "That pretty much sums it up."

"We must enjoy torturing ourselves," he says, although his head is down, and his keypad clicks as he types.

A car passes, pulling my attention.

Well, more like the writing on the side of the car pulls my attention.

Mashup Realty Co.

The car pulls into the driveway of the house next to me, and I watch to see who gets out. It's been a different employee each time they show the house. It's been on the market for four months now. I know, I know, coincidence, maybe? But they haven't had any takers yet, and I'm hoping that they don't until I finish a few more books. I need whatever momentum this house is giving me as it sits empty.

A woman gets out. Her hair is pinned up, and she's wearing a pantsuit.

Maybe my next heroine should sell houses, and when she goes to show one, there's a dead body. I grin. I love writing steamy romantic suspense. It's so different from the life I live that it gives me that reader's high of living a different life as I write.

The woman waves when she spots me watching.

"Maybe this is the one!" she yells.

I just force a smile.

"Let's hope not," I say under my breath. "Good luck!" I shout, and Tobias laughs.

"Would it be so bad to have a new neighbor? What if they have kids Grey's age? He'd love to have another kid on the street."

"That would be cool … at another house."

"Damn, you have really turned into a grump over the last year."

"No, I haven't."

"Oh, you have. Do you have too much on your plate? Can I help with anything to cheer you up?"

There is full sarcasm in his tone.

"I'm not grumpy, all right."

He grins. "Yeah. Sure. I should head out. I'm supposed to have dinner with Natalie."

I watch him as he packs up. These days, anytime he mentions Natalie, I get nervous for him. Especially since we all know her boyfriend bought her a ring. My heart is actually beating nervously for him. If he doesn't tell her how he feels before it's too late, I'm not so sure he can recover from that.

Before I can say anything about it though, someone rides by the house on their bike.

"Simon! Hey! Simon!"

I snap my attention to her and watch as she stops the bike next to the Realtor's car.

"Is that Greer?" Tobias asks.

"Yeah."

"Hey!" She waves again once she's off her bike and walks across the yard. "Are you two writing?"

"Well, my computer is in front of me, so I would say yes." Tobias kicks my leg.

"We were just finishing up, Greer. What are you doing?"

"Looking at this house," she says with a bright smile. "Wish me luck."

She turns and basically skips to the front door, waving one more time before she disappears through the door.

"Greer would be a great neighbor," Tobias says and jogs down the five steps off my porch.

"No, she wouldn't."

"Why not? She's super sweet. She's always in a great mood. Something you need."

"Yeah, she'd be nothing but a distraction and …" I let my words trail off when I spot my best friend grinning at me. "What?"

He shakes his head. "Nothing."

"What?" I ask again.

His hands go up. "I'll talk to you later."

"Tell me what you were going to say," I snap.

He just laughs and gets in his truck.

He pulls away from the curb and right as I turn around; I

spot Greer shaking hands with the Realtor through the front window. Then she claps and cheers, spinning in a circle.

Fuck.

Keep reading for a bonus epilogue!

BONUS EPILOGUE
12 YEARS LATER

Graham

I don't care what anyone says, looking at yourself on a poster or billboard is creepy. Look at how giant my face is. The arms are accurate I suppose, but the rest of me is … it's just weird. The poster in front of me is supposed to be life size, but it's taller than I am.

I glance at the floor, ah, it's on a platform.

Still, it's weird.

The fact they did a cut out of a picture of Paige and me together makes it a smidge better.

Paige's side of the poster looks fucking stunning, but I wouldn't expect anything less. That woman couldn't make a single picture look bad even if she tried. Hell, she tries to make faces all the time in family pictures just to make the girls laugh, but all I see is the funny, happy woman who I fell in love with, and I fall in love with her even more.

"Whoa, what is that?" Paige comes up behind me. She

244

slides one hand around my waist while the other rests on her baby bump.

The three girls back home with my sister make me a proud father, but the little boy who'll be here in a month or less is going to be the perfect addition to our family.

I wrap an arm around her shoulders. "That's going to haunt me forever," I say, pointing to mine. "And that one can come to the room with us later."

She shoves my chest on a laugh and turns to look at the room.

"I can't believe this is finally happening."

I turn to take it in for myself. Graham Wright has been to his fair share of book signings over the years, but today is different.

I've been writing under P.K. Lover since the day I signed with Vans as a steamy romcom writer, and not only did I see my bestselling Vans series on a billboard on the way here, but today, we're both revealing who P.K. Lover is and showing the opening scene to my first book that went to film.

It's a big day for me.

"Neither can I."

Who knew that the first steamy book I'd write twelve years ago for Vans Publishing House would lead to this? Not me, that's for sure.

"How long do we have until the doors open?" she asks, and Doug appears from around a shelf. The bookstore we're singing in today in Denver is modeled after a modern library. There are shelves everywhere and it's almost like a maze.

"Ten minutes. I'll go check to make sure everything is ready."

He disappears out the main doors and as soon as we're

alone, I pull Paige between two shelves where I know no one can see us.

I pull her close to me and press my lips to hers.

She responds with just as much desire, but when I try to slip my hand up her dress, she swats me away.

"And this is why we're about to have baby number four."

I laugh.

"It might also be why I have such great books. The heat is undeniable."

"You only have ten minutes," she says when I try to kiss her again.

"That's plenty of time."

"Graham Wright, you will keep your hands to yourself until we get to the room later, okay? Then you can be as wild as your heart desires."

I kiss her forehead and then hug her.

We stand there like this until Doug gives us a one-minute warning.

I take my seat, but Paige is at my side and as soon as the doors open, we both smile wide.

The first reader is in a full-blown wedding dress.

It makes sense since this book is about a runaway bride, after all.

I remember joking about turning our story into a book, and honestly, I don't think it'd be here without Paige telling me to do so.

We were sitting in the living room making a list, because if it wasn't on the list it didn't happen, during the first winter she was going to spend with me in Wind Valley. I told her I should write a story about us and make it my first steamy novel. She marched over to me with her notebook and pen, climbed into my lap, and said the three words that changed everything.

"Write that down."

What happens when you mix the small-town, grumpy single dad with the sunshine next door?

Find out in More Than Write!

Keep reading for a sneak peek!

MORE THAN WRITE

SNEAK PEEK

CHAPTER ONE
GREER

My ass hurts.

I pick up the fifty-pound kettlebell and proceed to squat for what feels like the hundredth time.

You like working out.

You're improving your mood.

You love food.

You have a pint of Cherry Garcia ice cream in the freezer.

Moving your body is good for you.

I repeat my mantra at least three more times as I finish my set. My current client is already lying on the floor, groaning.

"Hell, Greer," he says. "Day after day, you kill me while I'm here, and for some reason, I just keep coming back."

"Well, David, that's my job."

David owns the building where I work. It started as a health and nutrition studio that my best friend Willa opened, but as the spaces on either side of her studio slowly opened, she added them to her lease. When I told her I wanted to branch into personal training in addition to nutrition, she signed me on as partner, and after many trainings and certifications, here I am.

"Of all the people you could have chosen to work out with today, I can't believe you picked me," He laughs and rolls up to sit.

I take the spot next to him, sticking my legs out straight and reach for my toes.

I take part in at least one client's workout a day. I switch it up from time to time, since no two clients have the same workout.

"I needed a challenge today."

Did I really?

Yes and no.

I needed something to push me. To trick my brain into thinking of anything other than my personal life.

That's why I love what I do so much. I control the outcome when it comes to what goes in my mouth and my body movements. If I stick to the plan, it will work. The way I take care of my body is all up to me. Only me. Do I have days at home where I eat milk and cookies and vegetable fried rice takeout? Of course I do. I don't believe in cutting out food. I believe in balance. Even if it can be a real bitch sometimes to maintain.

Plus, David's workout was an hour compared to a lot of my thirty- or forty-five-minute clients, and today, I needed the full sixty minutes of distraction.

Unfortunately for me, it didn't matter if I had a fifty-pound weight on my thighs during my wall sits. The question on my mind still remains.

Why do men have to suck so damn bad?

It shouldn't be that hard to find a good guy.

I know they're out there. My best friends are living proof that they are. I've seen them in action. I've just yet had the chance to date one.

Honestly, there was one who came close. I even went as far as to take him to a work retreat once upon a time. But he claimed I was too intense for him. He wanted a laid-back life. Not one filled with goals and working out every day and precooked meals.

I get it. My lifestyle isn't for everyone. That's just fine. No two people are supposed to live the same life or have the exact same goals. We're meant to be different, but it does help if your partner gets you, supports you, and wants you to reach your goals even if they don't look like their own. That was my only boyfriend who gave me an actual reason—shit. This is exactly why I needed the full hour of self-torture. Once I get going on this mindset, I obsess over it.

I'm not boy crazy or man crazy or whatever you want to call it. I just want to find my person and make a life with him.

It sounds a lot simpler than it really is.

"Greer." David has moved on to the next stretch. He's even grabbed water from the cooler and is offering me one. "Is everything okay?"

"Yes," I answer and stand. "That one was a doozy."

I take the water and then grab my tablet to pull up my planner.

"Your wife comes in next. Did you want me to schedule the next few sessions as a joint one?"

Typically, I train only one client at a time, but the occasional couple doesn't bother me. Especially David and Melanie. They're a fun pair. They love a good challenge against one another.

"Yeah, but don't tell her. Let's keep it a surprise."

I smile and add those notes to my schedule. He packs up his things and leaves.

I sneak into the back of the studio to make a snack just as my phone goes off. It's a text reminder that my lawn guy is coming out tomorrow at eleven.

Shoot. I have a consultation for a new client at the same time, and I don't want to reschedule.

I also can't let the yard at my brand-new house die already either.

Despite my earlier pity party, I smile and do a little dance. Owning my own home was a big goal of mine, and I did it. All on my own.

I take a bite of my chocolate and cinnamon overnight oats. Who could possibly meet the lawn guy for me?

Willa is out of town. Calla, my other best friend, is just as busy with her own business, and Paige is visiting her brother. I bet Nora could do it.

I pull up her contact info and press the call button.

"Hey," she answers on the first ring. "I was just about to call you and change my appointment tomorrow morning."

"Is everything okay?" I grab my planner again.

"Yes, I just had a client call me with last-minute changes so tomorrow is going to be slammed."

Nora owns her own marketing company and specializes in working with authors. I know how important clients can be, so Nora is clearly out.

"Okay, no problem. I'll text you a few options for other openings I have this week, but it's pretty slim."

"You're the best. Now, what did you call for?"

"Oh, I have the lawn guy coming tomorrow, but I have a new client. I was going to see if you could meet him."

"Oh, I'm sorry, babe. Ask Simon. He's right there."

Ah, yes, my neighbor. He'll act like this small favor of letting someone into my backyard is a big inconvenience.

He's grumpy like that.

But Simon Stone is Calla's brother, and that's the only reason I'd even consider asking him.

"Yeah, I probably will. I just know he's busy."

"So are you. Honestly, he just has to open the gate for them. Ask him."

I could probably just leave the gate unlocked, but ick. It would drive me crazy all day knowing anyone could get into my space. I can't do it.

"I will."

"Okay, great. Let's get dinner and drinks as soon as everyone is back in town."

"Sounds great. Bye, Nora."

As soon as we hang up, I finish eating my midmorning snack and then glance at the clock. I have a lunch date, and if I leave now, that'll give me an hour to get ready with time to spare for visiting my neighbor. I'd call him, but we've only talked on the phone once, and that was months ago for his son, Grey. We'd met for dinner to go over some nutrition plans because Grey is getting into football and asked his dad if he could talk to a professional about the diet he should be on to set himself up for success. Honestly, it was the cutest thing. The fact we had this meeting at a restaurant that served unlimited chips and salsa was even better.

I push my bike, which I ride to and from work—downtown Wind Valley is only a ten-minute bike ride from my house—out the front door of the studio and lock up.

I remember that dinner like it was yesterday. Simon barely spoke. It was hard to get a word in with Grey talking and telling me all his goals for middle school and high school. He's only ten but talks like he's older. I loved that he has a plan and goals. Simon is very self-driven, so it makes sense that his kid is the same way. In the end, I gave him a few weeks of meal plan ideas, and we went our separate ways.

I'll have to ask Simon if those plans worked out for Grey.

I ride down Main Street, waving at a few random people before I turn onto the street that takes me back into the neighborhood where I live.

I wasn't born or raised in Wind Valley, but I went to college here and never left. Those people, the ones I don't even know who just waved at me, are the reason why. People here are just kind and friendly. It makes for a peaceful place to live.

The men though? Slim pickings.

However, I have high hopes for my lunch date. He's new to this area. I met him through an app, and he loves that I only schedule clients in the morning and the occasional evening, leaving my days open. Honestly, I didn't plan that from the beginning. I just have a lot of nine-to-five clients who can only train outside that, so thus, my schedule was created.

Still, his support on my out-of-the-ordinary schedule was nice. Obviously, that's not all I picked him on, but it was a perk.

I near my house, and my eyes trail in on my neighbor's front porch the way they always do.

Simon is sitting at his little white two-person table with

his laptop open in front of him and a glass of water next to it. Every day when I come home, he's in this spot. Laptop and water and all. I mean, it has to be water because it's a clear glass with clear liquid, and with his physique, I doubt he drinks much else besides a beer here or there at a friend's barbeque. Even though I wouldn't go as far to say Simon and I are friends, we do share a lot of them.

His gaze lifts from his laptop, and his eyes zero in on me.

"Hey, Simon." I smile and wave as I ride past his house. "It's so nice out today."

I hold my smile with confidence but cringe on the inside. I've said the same thing to him every day since I moved in a month ago. And each day when I ride by with my signature greeting, he just watches me without saying a word.

What a dick comes to mind, but I don't think that's the case. I don't know what his deal is, but I've seen him with Grey, and for as grumpy as Simon might be, I know deep down, he's hiding a pretty great person.

Gross. Listen to me. Is this because I just want to see the good in a single guy?

It has to be.

I park my bike in front of my garage door and walk up the sidewalk to my front door. I pause when Simon stands, his arms raising above his head as he stretches.

Now, our houses aren't kissing, but they are close enough for me to get a good view.

He's got his back to me, but his simple light gray shirt hugs his body in all the best ways. I can see the ripples of his upper back muscles, and I hate that I like it. I could get technical, but honestly saying *look at those trapezius and deltoids* doesn't sound as sexy.

Ugh, and the way his shirt hugs his biceps is great too. He flexes and the veins in his arms make an appearance. That's hot. He reaches just a little higher, and his shirt rises, revealing two dimples in his lower back. He's wearing sweats that are so perfectly low, if he turned around, I bet I'd see that V all the girls talk about.

Moody as he may be, Simon is easily the best-looking guy I've laid eyes on.

His arms drop and he sighs, one hand running through his thick black hair. He spins, sees me watching him, and pins his dark eyes on me.

What I would give to see a smile under that perfectly groomed scruff on his face.

He clears his throat.

I let out a bubble laugh and then disappear into my house.

So what if he caught me staring at him? I should probably feel guilty, but outside of his gorgeous appearance, he's not my type. Not to mention, he's never once shown any kind of interest in me. I'm clearly not his type either.

I smile.

I like to laugh.

I like conversation.

I jog up the stairs to my room and strip out of my leggings and sports bra and then get in the shower.

Enough hot neighbor talk. I have a date waiting for me, and I have a good feeling about this one.

CHAPTER TWO

SIMON

"Dad!"

I pull my gaze from the house next door, grab my computer and water, and head inside.

"Yeah?" I holler back to my ten-year-old son, Grey, who clearly can't be bothered to just walk outside to get me.

"We need to leave soon," he says, poking his head out of the kitchen, which is straight back from the front door at the back of the house. The living room is to the left, and the stairs that lead upstairs are to my right. Most of the houses in our neighborhood have the same layout. It's how I know that Greer, one of my sister's best friends who lives next door, has a house that mirrors mine. I also know this because it was on the market for so long that I toured it once to get ideas for the books I write.

I jog up the stairs to strip off my clothes to get ready. I'd been so into a zone this morning that as soon as I woke up and worked out, I'd gone right to the front porch to get some work done.

Steamy romantic suspense is my specialty, and something about having a house that wouldn't sell right next door to me sparked ideas for an entire six-book series. I went crazy with ideas and pitched them to my agent, who got me a signed deal within a few weeks. It helps that I've had bestsellers before and that I have a good relationship with all the publishing houses I've signed with. I've never missed a deadline, and as long as I'm in control, I won't ever.

It does, however, stress me out that I was so into a zone with the whole mystery house series that I agreed to closer deadlines when I signed the contract. Two months later, with four books of the series still left to write, the house was sold and that spark for the mysteriousness has dulled. Despite having a writing high this morning, that dull mood is not a good vibe for me right now.

Part of me thinks that if I could just get inside Greer's house and walk around alone, maybe that inspiration would come back. Like, maybe somehow, I could spin the type of person who moved into the house into the story. It would be nothing like Greer because her personality doesn't scream suspenseful. Her personality is more romcom. That's not my area.

With my fingers at the waist of my sweats, I start to tug them down, then movement out of my bedroom window catches my eyes.

Greer.

In a towel.

Until Greer moved in, I had no idea how much I'd see the woman whose bedroom window is right across from mine.

Right now, our houses aren't nearly far enough apart.

Her white towel is tied in a knot in front and her hair is up in a messy bun on top of her head as she opens drawer after drawer on her dresser, clearly undecided on what to wear.

Something more than skintight leggings and a crop top or sports bra, I hope.

I swear my mind and body can just sense when she's near, and as soon as that feeling hits me, I have no control over the way my eyes find her no matter what I'm doing.

It's why I'll never comment on the way I catch her checking me out. Like earlier. I'm not sure she's aware that she does this often when she's around me. But then again, I watch her like some weirdo every day when she rides her bike home, so I guess we've sort of called a silent truce of how we will never mention it to the other.

I let out a laugh as I step into the cold water.

Fucking hell.

Grey.

That kid takes half hour-long hot showers anytime I'm outside writing. I know he does.

Love the kid to death, but that's just unacceptable.

I wash quickly, wrap a towel around my waist, and head to my room to pick out clothes. Again, my eyes drift to the window.

There was only one other woman in my life who has ever stolen my attention the way Greer does.

Grey's mom. Blair.

We met before my twenty-first birthday, fell in love quickly, and she got pregnant all within about six months. I proposed a year or so after Grey was born, and then a week before Grey's second birthday, she left for the movies with friends. Next thing I knew, an officer was at our door to tell me about the car accident.

I hate that Grey has had to grow up without his mom. I hate that she never got to see him ride his first bike or hug him the first time he broke his arm. I hate that she never got her big day with the dress that's still packed away because what if Grey meets someone and she… fuck.

I take a breath and sit on the bed.

This right here, this feeling of knowing I had something amazing and lost it is why I've never seriously dated since Blair. Have I come to terms and accepted life without her? Yes. Am I thankful for every moment we had together? Yes. But loving someone and losing them is a feeling I never want to experience again.

"Dad!" Grey walks into my room.

"Hey, buddy. Knock first, remember?"

He groans and closes the door.

"Are you almost ready?" he yells from the other side instead of knocking.

I shake my head and grab some shorts and a shirt.

"Yep."

Then I slip on some sandals, brush my teeth, comb my hair, and open my door to find him waiting.

He looks at his watch.

"You're cutting it close," he says and leads me down the straight to the kitchen.

"We're going to make it just fine."

"Football starts at noon, and soccer is at three. I need to eat a proper amount of protein before then, Dad."

"Got it."

Hence why he's rushing me out the door. I promised him a power salad from one of the local juice shops downtown before practice today.

"No more pizza. We've had it three times this week."

"Okay, *Dad*," I tease and roll my eyes behind him. "Go get your things."

"They're already in the truck."

"Go brush your teeth then."

"Done." He smiles.

I glance around the clean kitchen, then I poke my head into the living room. There are actually vacuum lines in the carpet.

Damn. Okay. He can keep his half hour-long hot showers.

He grabs a water bottle from the cabinet and starts to fill it up at the fridge.

This single dad thing is tough shit sometimes, but I got lucky. Grey is a great kid.

"Stop staring at me," he whines, and then grabs his backpack before walking out the door to the garage.

I can't help but laugh.

Seriously, who is the parent here?

I hop into the truck, and as soon as we're both buckled in, I head downtown. It's a quick drive. The juice shop is four doors down from The Space, a community workspace location that Tobias and I just recently opened up.

We grab our salads and some juices before walking to The Space. There are a few spots open near the front window, so we take them.

I can't help but be impressed with this place.

It's been busy since we opened, and honestly, if I'm not writing on my porch, this is where I like to be.

"Hey," Tobias says when he walks in. His computer bag is slung over his shoulder. "Are you working today?"

Tobias and I met in college. In fact, that's how I met all

my friends. Tobias, Beck, Hero, Zane, Beck, and I all write romance, so it was easy for us to bond in college, since it isn't something a lot of guys choose as a career.

I shake my head to answer his question. "Just eating and relaxing before camp. I'll be back while he's there, though. My next book is due in two weeks, and the one after that is due in six."

Tobias whistles. "I can't believe you did that to yourself."

I was convinced the house next door wouldn't sell. A little too convinced. Clearly.

"Can you still meet the contractor this afternoon at three?" he asks.

"Yes."

"I have soccer, Dad." Grey cuts in.

"Oh, right." I look at Tobias. "Let's move it to four."

"You have to pick me up at four," Grey adds.

Shit.

"I can move something around," Tobias says. "I'll meet him today."

"Thanks."

Tobias and I have plans to open more locations around Wyoming. So things are crazy in all areas of my life. I'm not in denial. I know I spread myself thin.

"Dad, look, it's Greer," Grey says and points out the front window with his fork. Her bike rolls to a stop in front of the window, and she waves at us. Then she climbs off her bike, leans it against the building, and pushes the door open.

My eyes take in her white shoes, her lean tan legs, and then focus on the coral dress she's wearing that cinches at the waist and features a scoop neck. She has a small gold necklace with matching earrings, and her brown hair is down now, straight. Probably to accommodate the white bike helmet she's wearing. Her bright chocolate eyes catch mine for a moment before she looks between me and my son.

I swallow and then take another bite before I say something stupid, like how fucking sexy she looks right now.

"Hey, you two. You are the exact duo I was looking for."

"Is it to give us more meal plans?" Grey asks.

"No, but I can definitely do that this weekend."

"Cool." Grey smiles, and then goes back to his Game Boy and lunch.

"I was actually looking for you," she says.

I clear my throat and look up. "What do you need?"

"I need a favor tomorrow. The lawn in my backyard is dying fast and someone is coming to look at it. I was hoping you could let them in through the side gate. Or through the house since the gate lock can be a hassle sometimes."

I'll be honest, I was only half listening until she said *go through her house*. That's the kind of help I need right now.

"Yeah, I can do that."

"Really?" She beams. "It's not a problem?"

I shake my head and look at my salad. "Nope."

"Oh, great—here's my spare key."

Gold!

"I need to get going but thank you so much."

"You look really pretty. Where are you going?" Grey asks.

"Oh, thank you. I have a lunch date."

"She looks super pretty, huh, Dad?"

I turn my head slightly to glare at my kid but pull it together quickly.

"You do. Have fun."

Greer laughs and then winks at me. "Thanks, neighbor."

I watch as she walks over to the café catty-corner from us.

"Let's go, bud."

We finish our lunch, put it in the trash, and are headed to football camp when Grey speaks up.

"Oh no, I only packed my soccer shoes!"

"What?"

"We have to go home to get my cleats."

"We don't have time to grab them."

"Call Aunt Calla."

"Calla is busy, bud. Can't you just wear your soccer shoes?"

"No, I can't."

"Why not? They're both on the field, right?"

"It's not the same. I have to have different ones. Didn't you ever play sports in school, Dad?"

It takes all I have not to roll my eyes. I sure did. His persistence in having all the right equipment is me to a tee when I was his age.

"All right, well, you'll have to be late then."

"Hurry, Dad."

I head home, driving only five miles over, and Grey runs inside to grab his shoes. While I wait in the truck, a flash of coral and white goes by my rearview mirror.

I thought she had a lunch date.

I watch as Greer parks her bike, takes off her helmet, and walks up the sidewalk to her front door. She looks over for a split second. It's not much, but it's enough for me to see the tear sliding down her cheek. She swipes it away and goes inside.

My heart instantly clutches as I reach for the door handle.

I pause and take a breath.

Not my problem.

Not my problem.

Not my problem.

Grey comes running back and barely has the door open as he says, "Drive."

I laugh. I didn't know I was his getaway driver. But I wait for him to buckle up.

"You know what I was thinking," he says as I back out of the driveway.

"What's that?" I glance at Greer's house in the rearview mirror.

I bet her date was a jackass. Clearly he was if he made her cry. That right there is just another reason I won't ever date again. I've read some pretty bad first date stories. Hell, I've written them.

"You should get an assistant," Grey says matter-of-factly as he switches out his shoes.

"For what?"

"Lots of things. Your book stuff, me, the house, the food we eat. I like clean clothes too."

"I don't need an assistant, and I always wash your clothes."

"I still think you need one. Maybe your brain needs a break."

I'm about to reply when my agent calls, the ring pausing the radio and filling the speakers.

"Doug, hey," I answer through Bluetooth.

"Simon. How's it going?"

"Good. Just headed to Grey's first day of football camp."

"Fun. Fun. I'll make this quick. Did you happen to send

those first three chapters over last night? My emails have been acting up, so I wanted to check."

I groan.

"Nope. I forgot. I'll do it as soon as I drop Grey off and open my computer."

"Sounds good. Have fun, Grey."

"Thanks, Doug!"

The call ends, and I drum my thumb against the steering wheel.

How did I forget to send those chapters?

"See?" Grey smiles at me in the rearview mirror. "An assistant could have helped you remember that."

I nod but don't say anything.

He might be onto something.

MORE BOOKS BY JAMI ROGERS

For the full list of titles by Jami Rogers, please scan the QR code below.

ACKNOWLEDGMENTS

Having a team who is always there for you when you write and release a new book is gold for an author. Julie, Hang Le, Jenny, and Dana are my team. Without them, these books would be a lot harder to write. I've said it before, but am truly lucky to have you all on this journey with me.

Of course, can't forget about my girl Brix. I started the first book in this series one afternoon during her nap time. We were camping and she was a baby *baby* who I did not want to leave alone in the camper. It didn't matter that everyone was sitting in chairs outside the door and could hear if she made a noise, I was right there next to her writing a new book on my phone. Here we are four books later.

As always, thank you to my husband for listening to me talk about these stories and the process day in and day out. Sometimes, plot holes are fixed by talking about them out loud and I'm not sure you understand how much you help by just listening.

THANK YOU to my ARC team. Having you has been a game-changer. Having you on my team for my last release was so much fun. I have a feeling it will be even better from here on out. You are the best!

Thank you to all the readers who read, share, and enjoy my stories. You motivate me more than you will ever know.

Cheers to the next book!

ABOUT THE AUTHOR

My name is Jami Rogers, and I write slow-burn contemporary romance novels. I *love* love and want to share my passion for happily ever afters with the world.

I was born in Wyoming and still live in the cowboy state with my husband, daughter, and dog. I like to read, write, run, watch movies/TV, and spend time with my family. I'm horrible at returning phone calls and prefer to text, but still struggle to hit the little blue arrow to send a message once I'm finished typing my reply. My husband does 90% of the cooking in our house. Not because I'm busy – I'm just simply a bad cook.

www.authorjamirogers.com

Want more from Jami?
Subscribe to her mailing list for exclusive bonus epilogues, giveaways, and all the book news!

www.ingramcontent.com/pod-product-compliance
Lightning Source LLC
Chambersburg PA
CBHW061232310726
48971CB00007B/2030